Jane Gardam has won two Whitbread awards (for *The Queen of the Tambourine* and *The Hollow Land*). She was also shortlisted for the Booker Prize with *God on the Rocks*, which was made into a much-praised TV film. She is a winner of the David Higham Award and the Royal Society of Literature's Winifred Holtby Prize for her short stories about Jamaica, *Black Faces, White Faces*, and *The Pangs of Love*, another collection of short stories, won the Katherine Mansfield Award. *Going into a Dark House* won the Macmillan Silver Pen Award. In 1999 she was awarded the Heywood Hill Literary Prize for a lifetime's commitment to literature.

Jane Gardam was born in Coatham, North Yorkshire. She lives in a cottage on the Pennines and in East Kent, near the sea.

JANE GARDAM

Bilgewater

An *Abacus* Book

First published in Great Britain by
Hamish Hamilton Ltd in 1976
Published by Abacus in 1985
This edition published by Abacus in 1997
Reprinted 1998, 2000, 2001, 2003 (twice)

ISBN 0 349 11402 1

Printed and bound in Great Britain by Clays Ltd, St Ives plc

Abacus
An imprint of
Time Warner Books UK
Brettenham House
Lancaster Place
London WC2E 7EN

www.TimeWarnerBooks.co.uk

for
WP + V^A × 47
1918–1965

"Youth is a blunder."
         Disraeli.

                  "Now –
counter to the previous syllogism:
tricky one, follow me carefully, it
may prove a comfort?"

                  Tom Stoppard
        (*Rosencrantz and Guildenstern*
                are Dead)

Prologue

THE INTERVIEW seemed over. The Principal of the college sat looking at the candidate. The Principal's back was to the light and her stout, short outline was solid against the window, softened only by the fuzz of her ageing but rather pretty hair. Outside the bleak and brutal Cambridge afternoon – December and raining.

The candidate sat opposite wondering what to do. The chair had a soft seat but wooden arms. She crossed her legs first one way and then the other – then wondered about crossing her legs at all. She wondered whether to get up. There was a cigarette box beside her. She wondered whether she would be offered a cigarette. There was a decanter of sherry on the bookcase. It had a neglected air.

This was the third interview of the day. The first had been as she had expected – carping, snappish, harsh, watchful – unfriendly even before you had your hand off the door handle. Seeing how much you could take. Typical Cambridge. A sign of the times. An hour later and then the second interview – five of them this time behind a table – four women, one man, all in old clothes. That had been a long one. Polite though. Not so bad. "Is there anything that *you* would like to ask *us*?"

("Yes please, why I'm here. Whether I really want to come even if you invite me. What you're all like. Have you ever run mad for love? Considered suicide? Cried in the cinema? Clung to somebody in a bed?")

"No thank you. I think Miss Blenkinsop-Briggs has already answered my questions in the interview this morning." They move their pens about, purse their lips, turn to one another from the waist, put together the tips of their fingers. I look alert. I sit upright. I survey them coolly but not without respect. I might get in on this one. But don't think it is a good sign when they're nice to you, said old Miss Bex.

And now, here we are. The third interview. Meeting the Principal. An interview with the Principal means I'm in for a Scholarship. How ridiculous!

I can't see her face against the light. She's got a brooding shape. She is a mass. Beneath the fuzz a mass. A massive intelligence clicking and ticking away – observing, assessing, sifting, pigeonholing. Not a feeling, not an emotion, not a dizzy thought. A formidable woman.

She's getting up. It has been delightful. She hopes that we may meet again. (Does that mean I'm in?) What a long way I have come for the interview. The far far north. She hopes that I was comfortable last night.

We shake hands in quite a northern way. Then she puts on a coat – very nice coat, too. Fur. Nice fur. Something human then about her somewhere. She walks with me to the door and down the stairs and we pause again on the college steps.

There is a cold white mist swirling about, rising from the river. The trees lean, swinging long, black ropes at the water. A courtyard, frosty, of lovely proportions. A fountain, a gateway. In the windows round the courtyard the lights are coming on one by one. But it's damp, old, cold, cold, cold. Cold as home.

Shall I come here?

Would I like it after all?

Chapter 1

MY MOTHER died when I was born which makes me sound princess-like and rather quaint. From the beginning people have said that I am old-fashioned. In Yorkshire to be old-fashioned means to be fashioned-old, not necessarily to be out of date, but I think that I am probably both. For it is rather out of date, even though I will be eighteen this February, to have had a mother who died when one was born and it is to be fashioned-old to have the misfortune to be and look like me.

I emerged into this cold house in this cold school in this cold seaside town where you can scarcely even get the telly for the height of the hills behind – I emerged into this great sea of boys and masters at my father's school (St Wilfrid's) an orange-haired, short-sighted, frog-bodied ancient, a square and solemn baby, a stolid, blinking, slithery-pupilled (it was before they got the glasses which straightened the left eye out) two-year-old, a glooming ten-year-old hanging about the school cloisters ("Hi Bilgie, where's your broomstick?") and a strange, thick-set, hopeless adolescent, friendless and given to taking long idle walks by the sea.

My father – a Housemaster – is known to the boys as Bill. My name is Marigold, but to one and all because my father is very memorable and eccentric and had been around at the school for a very long time before I was born – I was only Bill's Daughter. Hence Bilgewater. Oh hilarity, hilarity! Bilgewater Green.

I will admit freely that I very much like the name Marigold.

Marigold Daisy Green is my true and christened name and I think it is beautiful. Daisy was my mother's name and also comes into Chaucer. Daisy, the day's-eye, the eye of day, (*The Legend of Good Women*, Prologue l.44) as my dear Uncle Edmund Hastings-Benson now and then reminds me (he teaches English as well as Maths). It seems to me a great bitterness that anyone with a name so beautiful as Marigold Day's-eye Green should be landed with Bilgewater instead however appropriate this may be. "In the end," says somebody, "almost everything is appropriate", and indeed the boys over the years have had a peculiar flair for hitting on the right word for a nick-name.

Nick-name. Old Nick's name. Bilgewater.

Bilgewater Green.

My father and I live alone in his House except for about forty boys who live on the Other Side through a green door and along a corridor with Paula Rigg the matron. Our side – father's and mine – is called the Private Side and we share it only with a cat or two and Mrs Thing who comes in and does for us. Mrs Thing changes from time to time and the cats vary as cats do and the boys arrive and pass by and depart like waves in the sea, but father and I and Paula are constant. Paula has been matron on the Other Side for as long as I can remember.

I am at the local Comprehensive. I don't eat at home at all in term-time with my father as he takes Boys' Breakfast and I have a hunk and a gulp at the kitchen table before I take myself off along the promenade to school, eat lunch there and have a tray of supper in my room prepared by Mrs Thing if she remembers or if I'm lucky by Paula while father takes Boys' Supper in Hall. But even if father and I don't eat together and I am out of the House for most of the day and he has Prep. and Private Coaching for part of most evenings we spend most of the rest of our days together and usually in utter silence.

For if I am Bilgewater the Hideous, quaint and barmy, my father is certainly William the Silent. Except when he is teaching he is utterly quiet. Even when he is teaching he never, so I'm told, has to raise his voice. He is amazed to hear of new masters with sweaters and fizzy hair cuts who smoke in class and have trouble keeping discipline. He shakes his head over this. He scarcely speaks at all. He moves so quietly about the House that you never know which room he's in. You will walk into his study and he'll just be standing there, perhaps looking down at the chess board, or up at the Botticelli Head of Spring above the fireplace or sitting with a cat on his knee looking out at the garden. He never rustles, coughs or hums. He never snuffles (thank goodness) and he never, ever, calls out or demands anything. If Paula comes in and puts a cup of tea down beside him he looks up at her and smiles as if that is what he has most yearned for: yet he would never ask. His peacefulness is everywhere he goes – in the House and out of it. He has not the faintest idea that I am ugly and we are very happy together.

The Greens of course are thought to be odd and father's silence and my ugliness and the lack of what is called a social life is much remarked upon. In the holidays my father likes a school empty of boys and so we have hardly ever gone away. At my school I make no friends and have always sat and set off home again alone. I am hopeless at games and have joined no clubs. All the other girls who live in streets or estates around the town have always seemed to be in ready-made groups and gangs, and from the beginning, because of my eyes, I have always had to sit in the front of the form-room just below the mistress's desk, which is not popular territory. I have for years stayed in at Breaks, too – we are allowed: it is Free Expression – because for ages I didn't seem able to pass the time out of doors in the playground. Later on, when I could read it was easier, but it is not often warm enough on this part of the Yorkshire coast to read for long out of doors.

There was a girl once I got on with – the Headmaster's daughter at father's school. She was around for a bit when I was very little – a funny girl. But she went off to boarding school and the Headmaster has a house in France and a mother in Wiltshire. They get out of the North as fast as they can in the holidays. I've not seen her for years.

Let me describe how it is with me and father.
I drift in from school.
"Hullo father."

"Ah."

I put down my homework and walk about his study for a while. I find myself beside the fireside stool where the chess is out. I stand and regard the chessmen. After a while I move something and time passes. Boys clatter by outside. My father sits – working or reading. Or sits.

"I've moved a bishop."

"You've moved a *bishop*?"

Time passes.

My father comes across and regards the board from the opposite side. He says, "Ah."

We stand.

Then he sits down still looking at the board. Then I sit down still looking at the board. At last he says, "So you've moved a bishop?"

Then spring, pounce, he moves a pawn and we sit.

After a while I say, "Oh hell."

"Ha."

"That's it then."

"Hum."

"Isn't it? It's check? It's – "

"Well – "

"It's mate."

"No. No. *Think*, Marigold."

Again silence. There is at length the clanging jamboree of the Prep. bell or the supper bell, or a boy arrives with an O level test paper or old Hastings-Benson puts his huge red face around the door and away my father goes.

I believe that father's friends are considered almost as odd as we are and Hastings-Benson (HB = Pencil, dimin.Pen. "In the end all things are appropriate", ibid.) perhaps the oddest. He is certainly the nicest.

He is old – generations older than father – and a Captain in the army in some War or other father was too young for. He won a lot of medals there and then went to Cambridge and became a Senior Wrangler. He is thus – or was – more brilliant even than my father who would never wrangle with anyone. He is a very big man even now and must have been a giant before he went to the trenches

14

years and years ago and got gassed. It is the gas and the trenches, Paula says, that did for him and has resulted in his high shoulders and visits to The Lobster Inn every night along the sea-front these fifty years or so. "You're so lucky," visitors say, visiting from the major public schools. "He's *brilliant*. Could have gone anywhere." And in spite of The Lobster Inn his results are still pretty good and everyone's so fond of him that it would be a great pity if he did go anywhere. Mind you at nearly eighty he's not likely to go anywhere much now.

His great friend is Puffy Coleman (History) who always stands sideways in the School Photograph because his teeth drop out. The Headmaster said at the last one, "Let's see, Coleman – how many School Photographs is this for you?"

"Thirty, Headmaster. Perhaps thirty-one."

"Then what about a full face this year? Quite solemn, you know. No need to smile."

But Mr Coleman after a lot of pondering and swinging about in his gown which is green as grass and has buttercups and the eyes of day sprouting out of the seams and dates from the time of St Wilfrid the Founder – Mr Coleman swings about, rotates his jaw a bit as is his wont before utterance and says, "No, Headmaster. Not this year. I think not," and does his usual click-toes left-turn, appearing as usual peering deeply into Hastings-Benson's right ear with his nose almost touching the tassel. The tassel that is to say of Hastings-Benson's mortar-board because my father's school is immensely out of date, dresses to kill and stands on ceremony and Hastings-Benson stands higher on ceremony than most. He has stood on ceremony for so long that he has come to symbolise the school in the four corners of the earth – perhaps rather further in these days now that the Empire is over and the Commonwealth a shadow – but still he is remembered. On various nostalgic occasions when Old Boys are gathered together they will talk of their schooldays and say, "Remember old Hastings-Benson?" And they will all start to roar and laugh.

It seems to me that Uncle Edmund Hastings-Benson has served his country well if someone, twenty, thirty years on can say, "D'you remember him?" and roar and laugh. Such a man is an immortal, a god come down. In fact let me state boldly that if I had to choose between Hastings-Benson and a god come down, full ankle deep in lilies of the vale (Keats. Paula) it would be Hastings-Benson for me every time. I love him. We understand each other. He is far from dead yet.

I will tell you why they laugh at him: he is always falling in love. My mother was his first and everyone apparently said then, no wonder for she was such a beauty. "That wonderful hair. And really — married to poor old Green!" In fact however I don't believe my mother loved Uncle Edmund at all — or just as everybody does. As I do — for I have been told that my mother adored my father, poor and old though he may seem, and my father for all these seventeen years has never looked at another woman. He keeps her photograph by his bed where it has turned the colour of white coffee and very soft and faded. You can't see much of her really but the hat which is floppy with a rose in it, a string of amber beads, and a lovely gentle chin not in the least like mine.

My mother fairly set Uncle HB off and all my life I have known that we have to be kind to him because he's sad. Love has always made him sad. It's odd he has kept at it so assiduously when you come to think of it. On and on he goes however — first it's the girl in the chemist in the town, then it's the new woman on school dinners, then it's the terrible 'cellist they got in for the school orchestra, then it's the Pro they took in for the school Christmas production of *Captain Brassbound's Conversion*. That one was a tremendous do — just last year — and I was in at every phase of it because Mrs Bellchamber — the actress in question — stayed in our House and Uncle Edmund was round morning, noon and night, leaving his classes, forgetting the Scholarship Sixth, abandoning the second eleven and you could hear the noise from his Silent Study right over on to Scarborough promenade. The reason being that he was nowhere near it being over in the school theatre ostensibly supervising the lighting for the first night, which is why the whole stage, auditorium and half the High Street was plunged into darkness and a quiet, able boy called Boakes who really knows something about lighting was flung to the floor from a ladder with such a charge of electricity through him that he will be safe from rheumatism to the second and third generation if such, and no thanks to Uncle Edmund, he manages to produce.

When this actress left, Uncle Edmund's plight was pitiable. He pinned people down, he pressed them against walls to talk about it. Paula would put her head round father's study door when we were deep in chess and cry, "Run — he's coming!" and my father would be out of the back door and hiding in the Fives Court. Once when Uncle HB was very desperate he went off to see Puffy Coleman — the one who stands sideways — and when he found the door locked, the front door and the back door, too, he went round to Mr Coleman's back shed — I suppose he guessed Mr Coleman had seen him coming and had gone up to bed and down under the blankets though it was mid-afternoon and a warm Spring. He took a ladder out of Mr Coleman's shed and put it up against the back wall of Mr Coleman's house. Mr Coleman said that it was most unpleasant and eerie to hear the clump clump of the ladder getting into position and the scraping on the wall, and the two spikes of ladder appear between his bedroom curtains and the bounce and creak of Uncle Edmund Hastings-Benson's mounting feet. Deeper down beneath the sheets he went as Uncle E.HB's great big red face and huge hook nose and kind little blue eyes rose like the dawn behind the pane and tap tap tap — "I say, Coleman. Will you let me in? I'm afraid I really must talk to you. It's about Mrs Bellchamber."

Thus I have been no stranger to love, isolated though my life has been. The derangement love seems to cause has actually made me value isolation more as term has followed term.

And I love the holidays.

Let me describe how it is with me and father in the school holidays.

My father is reading in the Fives Court and looks up to see if I am still there. When he sees that I am not, he wanders about in the rockery, then among the greenhouses and lettuce beds to see if I am there, keeping his fingers all the time in the place in the text — he teaches the Classics and reads them all the time for pleasure, too. On the journey he gets deflected once or twice, standing for long stretches of time regarding a caterpillar negotiating a stone, picking a sweet-pea and running a finger up and down its rough, ridgy stalk, walking out to the village shop to buy tobacco but forgetting the tobacco to watch water running down a drain. At most seasons of the year he wears long mufflers curled over into tubes. He has an invalidish look, fragile at the waist, snappable as a sweet-pea and this is for some reason lovable. If he notices anybody as he walks about he smiles at them and they look at him kindly back.

Sometimes he finds me. If it is summer he most likely finds me in the School pool, swimming up and down. It is one of the most marvellously royal and luxurious things to do – most princess-like – to be legitimately and all alone in a school swimming pool in the school holidays. Up and down, up and down I swim, frog's face, frog's body, eyes shut tight, thinking how I would be the envy if they knew it of the whole of my Comprehensive who are all in the town making do with the Public Baths or the freezing sea.

Up and down, up and down I swim, father standing across on the shore, like Galilee, watching the green water and the black guide lines wriggling like snakes as I pass over them. "There's a poor beetle," he calls. "Whisk it out. That's right. Poor fellow."

Up and down the pool I go, spluttering bubbles. Soon my father starts reading again. After a while, still reading he wanders away.

Once – just once – when I was about thirteen I remember opening my eyes and finding him gone and wondering in a very inconsequential way if my mother had had a rather unexciting life.

Chapter 2

THROUGHOUT THE peace there has always of course been Paula and perhaps without Paula such peace would have been intolerable. Perhaps it was intolerable, it occurs to me now. Perhaps that is why my mother upped and died. Perhaps my mother took one look at me and thought, "I'm bored stiff and now *this*." I think that it may be Paula who makes desirable the wonderful peacefulness of father, and the great tornado of Paula which makes the still air round father such delight.

She is thirty-six and comes from Dorset. That in itself is extraordinary for up here. You meet plenty of people in the North-East from Pakistan or Jamaica or Uganda or Zambia or Bootle but scarcely a body from the south coast of England.

Paula arrived here mysteriously – I don't think she had thought it all properly out – when she was seventeen as assistant to a real matron who retired hastily leaving Paula to swoop into power. She must have looked and been most improperly young but I would like to see the Headmaster or Board of Governors or representative of any Ministry of Education, Emperor, Principality or Power who could have removed her even at seventeen had she a mind to stay. And not a gestapo, K.G.B. nor any hosts of Midianites I think would ever have wanted Paula to go. Once you've met her you need her. The world runs down, the lights go out and everyone starts stumbling in the dark the minute Paula isn't there.

She's lovely, Paula. She has a grand straight back joining on to a long, duchess-like neck and a whoosh of hair scooped into a silky high bundle with a pin. She's tall, with a fine-drawn narrow figure with sloping shoulders and whatever she wears looks expensive. At father's school functions she sails in dressed in anything and sits down anywhere and all eyes turn. She nods and smiles, this way and that, and all the pork butchers' wives in polyester and earrings on the platform look like rows of dropping Christmas trees.

Paula has a voice like *Far from the Madding Crowd* – beautiful. "There's my duck," "That's my lover." To show you the full marvellousness of Paula when she says, "That's my lover" to any of the boys who's in her sick room I've never heard of one who sniggered.

Paula's deep funny burry voice goes with her rosy cheeks and bright eyes and hurtling feet. She is always running and usually towards you. "Oh for a beaker full of the warm South," always makes me think of Paula, and I told her so the first time she read it to me when I was about eleven. I was a very late reader and it was an effort even at eleven to sit down and read for long so Paula used to read to me. I wish she did so still.

"Warm south," says Paula, "Wish I wurr an' not in this God-forzaken hoale."

"Why d'you stay here then?" asks the boy of the day, calling through from the sick room. There is a sick room for solitary sufferers and a San for epidemics. The sick room nearly always has someone or other in it, usually one of the youngest ones. They troop up in droves. "Matron, I'm sick," "Matron, I've got a burst appendix," "Matron, I've punctured a lung," and she bundles them off whizz, bang, thermometer, pulse – "Rubbish, my lover. Stop it now, do. Sit through on the bed and drink some cocoa and hush whilst I read to our Marigould." She sorts them out every time, the ones who are sick and the ones just home-sick. They say terrible things sometimes.

"Matron, I'm bleeding from the ears."

"Matron, Terrapin's committed suicide."

"Matron, Boakes is in a coma."

If it's not true, and it hardly ever is – she knows. If it is true she's like a rushing mighty wind and the local hospital is on its toes in an instant as she hurtles down upon it ahead of the stretcher, orderlies toppling like ten-pins, the plume of hair bouncing masterfully to the very lintel of the operating theatre door. She's well-known is Paula. When anyone is waiting for exam results it is Paula who prises them out. She's down at the Post Office at dawn. They expect her now. And when there is any trouble or excitement in a boy's family she knows the minute it has happened, and sometimes before.

"Why d'you stay here?" asked the patient of the day after I'd told her she was like the warm South.

"The dear knows, my lover."

"Who's the dear?" asked the boy. It was probably Terrapin or Boakes. They were forever slurping cocoa the first year or so.

"Well, not you and that's for sure."

Terrapin (or Boakes) lay comfortably warm within, just out of sight through the sick-room door. I sat on the floor by Paula's sitting room fire. Paula sat in the rocking chair, straight upright under her hair, Keats on her knee.

"Full of the true, the blushful Hippocrene."

The fire blazed up. There was a raw, bleak wind outside and a black branch tap-tapping on the glass, sea-gulls shouting miserably at each other, the sea noisy. On the mantelpiece was a picture of Paula's family – a farmer on a hay-cart and a lot of little children grinning and squinting against the sun in floppy hats. Somewhere near Lyme Regis apparently, wherever that was. Dorset. Wessex. The warm South.

"Why d'you stay here, Paula?"

"Because you're always askin' for stories," Paula said. "I've been taken kind-hearted. Seems to me I'm a very nice woman."

She went on with the *Ode to a Nightingale* and Terrapin – I remember now that it was Terrapin – made faces at me of peculiar horror from the sick-room bed, leaning out of it from the knees so he could see me and looking fit as a flea.

I never felt that Paula found me very important though. Far from it. She never had favourites. There is a great sense of irrevocable justice about her and although one had the sensation that her devotions and emotions ran deep and true you never found her ready to discuss them – not the loving emotions anyway.

21

Whether it were ridiculous Terrapin, friendly Boakes or wonderful divine and heavenly Jack Rose, the hero of the school, she treated them all alike. For me she had had from the start a steady unshakeable concern that wrapped me round like a coat. She never fussed me or hung about me and since I was a little baby I don't remember her ever kissing me or hugging me. Every night of my life she has looked in on me at bedtime to tuck me in, and when I had the measles or the chicken pox I had them over in the Boys' Side with her and I knew absolutely for certain though I never asked that she would always be within call.

But she has never tried to mother me. She's not a soft woman, Paula. She cannot stand slop of any kind and again and again she says — it is her dictum, her law unquestionable — BEWARE OF SELF PITY.

Yet you can tell her anything. She is never shocked, she is never surprised. She accepts and accepts and accepts. Puffy Coleman keeps falling in love with the very little boys ("Well, it's not as if he *does* anything"); dear Uncle Edmund Pen HB climbs ladders and weeps for love of anything vaguely female ("He's romantic the dear knows"); one of the boys gets howling drunk at The Lobster Inn after failing all his O levels ("He's to be sobered and pitied and set to do them again at Christmas"). And she never thought that it was in any way odd that I could not read at the age of ten. "If the eyes are right," she said, "and we have now got them right, the reading will come. I've no opinion of these mind-dabblers and I.Qs. and dear knows." And the reading did come. In the end.

And Paula never, ever, gives me the impression that I am ugly and once when I said something of the kind she went off like a bomb. "You get no sympathy from me on that score, my lover," she declared, thumping and clattering about with a sewing-machine.

"I've no friends," I wailed. (It was after the measles. I was in a bad way.)

"More fool you."

"Everyone hates me."

"Don't be conceited. Oh help me and save me the thing is all busted to bits."

"Not surprising when you've dropped it on the floor. That was my *mother's* sewing-machine," I said. I remember I took pleasure in saying this. I intoned it. "My father gave it to my mother. She always loved it."

"Pity she didn't use it a bit more then. To think when I came here and you a naked worm wrapped in old bits of blanket and not a gown prepared!"

"She was unworldly — "

"Then she's best off where she is."

"Paula!"

"BEWARE OF SELF PITY," she thundered, bright-eyed and beautiful, "BEWARE OF — "

"I've no mother. I can't read. I'm ug — "

"You can read as well as many. You're a witch at your figures. You can play difficult piano by ear and you can keep up with your father at his chess. What's more — "

"I'm ugly."

"You've got lovely skin and hands and hair."

"Oh Paula, my hair's terrible. It's frizzy. It's fluorescent. It gives you a migraine. It's the joke of the place."

"You wait," said Paula, solemn as an oracle, sticking the needle of the sewing-machine through her little finger and out the other side and bellowing like a beast, "I'm injured, I'm bleeding, I'm stuck to the needle!"

Rescued, rocking herself, she added, "You're the best girl in the world. You're the best friend in the world."

"Well, you're mine too I suppose," I said and we looked at each other, no nonsense. Then I said, "Actually you're the only friend, just as I'm yours. We haven't got any more."

"That's true," said Paula clutching her hand up into a ball and sitting on it to kill off the pain, "This god-forsaken loanely place."

"Well why d'you stay here?"

Which was where we began.

Thursdays were always the evenings when these conversations with Paula took place and had done so "from long since" as our Mrs Things say, because Thursdays were the evenings when father received visitors.

He had done this since before the war, even before he was married, and the visitors had always been the same: one or two, never more than three Old Masters. Uncle Pen and Puffy Coleman were inevitables and the third was often an amalgam of cobwebs and dust called Old Price. Every term-time Thursday at about seven-thirty these people came roaming round like elderly, homing snails. They unwind garments in the hall when it is not cold, drop walking sticks – Uncle HB has a shooting stick – into the hall-stand and trail dismally into the study. Paula takes them coffee and glasses and father slowly unlocks the shelf-cupboard in the bottom of his desk and brings out a bottle of wine which he never opens until well after they have all arrived and would probably never open at all if he were not kept very firmly at it by Uncle HB who often brings a personal hip-flask, too, though I don't think father has ever noticed.

Uncle HB as the minutes after the coffee wear on thumps the hip-flask about and moves it into very conspicuous places because he is a good man and loathes cowardice of all kinds and believes in straightforward honesty where weaknesses are concerned. "I drink," he says, "but never secretly", and he glares round the room as if everybody else has a still in the wardrobe. My father doesn't drink secretly either and I'm sure Puffy doesn't – only lots of ginger beer with the boys – and if Old Price drank more than two sips he'd go up in a little wisp of smoke. I often wonder how the convention of father providing the wine began and why he is expected to produce a weekly bottle of what Paula calls Rosy when he seems to need so very few of the usual pleasures of life. On his own he would never get any further than the mechanics of gazing at the bottle and peering about under exercise books, old tea pots and the odd sock for the corkscrew and at long last, standing like a priest at Mass gazing at the pinkness of the wine held aloft towards the window or the slinky, chilling sexy face of Primavera over the fireplace. In the end Uncle Pen who never notices the colour or the Botticelli takes the bottle from him, smells it, complains of it and pours it out. Paula then leaves them, taking the tray, and the four of them sit on until about half-past ten.

Sometimes, when I was little I was allowed to sit with them for a bit – well, not so much allowed. I just did. They did not seem to notice and I learned much. When I was four or five I would sit for ages under the desk playing with a heap of old shoes my father keeps there. They were friendly shoes with names and I had good long private conversations with them before Paula descended like a valkyrie. "Now excuse me of course and such-like, but she's 'ere and I'm 'avin' 'er out. Under that desk. Yes. I've looked the school over. Ought to be 'shamed! She'll be stunted of growth. Five year old and after eight o'clock at night! No don't disturb yourself Mr Hastings. Hold on to your flask it'll topple" – and her arms would come scooping down and gather me up and I'd be flown through the air above all their heads, yelling "I'm not *tired*. I'm busy. You're not KIND Paula," etc., dangling by its laces a shoe which would never see home or family again.

As I grew older I became too large to fit under the desk and also if I may be forgiven for mentioning it, the smell down there was getting a bit on the fruity side, and I abandoned the Thursday receptions for Paula's sick bay readings and learned there much more interesting, universal and philosophic things.

I have read novels now full of intelligent conversations. In novels there is often a set-piece thrown in called The University or College Conversation. This can take place between students or long afterwards, in the evenings of the students' days. There are a great many pauses in it and as the pipe smoke rises and the firelight flickers on the rows of mellow old volumes, wisdom and gentle nostalgia hang in the air. The nature of God, the reality of solid objects, the non-existence of Time are touched upon, tossed gently to and fro. Not so with father's lot. Up with Paula, the floor above – and Paula has had no education at all – we talk on and on about:

> sin
> death
> love
> harmony
> ethics

particularly ethics, e.g. when Posy Robinson comes in all tearful for his mama and we have only two eggs and two rashers and two spoons of cocoa, our four feet on the fender and a lovely play coming on the wireless after the news.

But downstairs! Here is a sample of the chat on one of the

Learned Thursdays:

"Cold night."

"Rather better."

"Pretty cold. Got your coal yet?"

"No. Got your oil?"

"No!"

"Time this House had oil. No more expensive."

"Smells."

"Not at all. No shovelling what's more."

"Your House has a Man."

"Man! Idle oik. If we got oil we could get rid of him."

"Get rid of Gunning? Get rid of *Gunning?*"

"'Bout time. Been here since the zeppelins."

Uneasy pause while it is considered whether Old Price has been here since the zeppelins.

"I once saw the zeppelins," says Puffy Coleman kindly. "I was just a boy. There was a burst of flame out over the sea — off Scarborough and then we saw a lot of little flames dropping into the water. Little flaming men. That was a terrible war."

"Terrible."

"What was terrible?"

"That war."

"Which war?"

"Well — the Last War. The — zeppelin war."

"I can remember," says a very feeble voice in the corner if it is a warm evening — he comes on chosen evenings, Old Price, like Masefield's blackbird — "I can remember the zeps. All the boys ran out along the cliff tops cheering. In their pyjamas."

"Ah," says Puffy Coleman, lowering his teeth.

"Ah," says Uncle Pen HB. Then, "It wasn't *that* war."

"Yes it was. What d'you think it was? The Napoleonic War?"

"Scarborough was bombarded in the Napoleonic War," whispers Old Price.

"Now then Price, you weren't in the Napoleonic War," says Pen.

"No. No. I only said — uff, uff, uff — "

Father gazes at the uplifted wine. The Primavera watches through her wicked eyes.

"D'you think Price was in the Napoleonic War, William?"

"What's that?"

"Uff, uff, uff – "

"Ha, ha, ha, ha," says father, bewildered, looking round sweetly, kindly at one and all, not at all sure, for he is a good bit younger than the others, what might or might not be so.

They reflect.

Oh it's wild stuff.

Chapter 3

WHAT ALL THIS rigmarole is meant to lead up to is the fact that although I had spent, quaintly and princess-like, so much of my life among people years and years older than myself and knew something about the peculiarities of grown-ups, I knew absolutely nothing about myself and others of my age and this is what made the first revelations when they came so unnerving.

There were two of these in particular and they were several years apart, not dramatic or exciting to anybody else but a swarm of troubles and misconceptions and shynesses and agonies sprang out of them.

Both of them were to do with the boy Terrapin.

The first was when I was thirteen and I was sitting in my bedroom towards the end of summer quite late one evening. It was still light – one of the occasional northern summer nights when it doesn't ever get completely dark at all and you remember that Norway is only a few hundred miles away, nearer than Cornwall. It was a night as warm as Cornwall, light, shadowy, soft, not heavy or thundery; a basking, sleepy, scented night that makes you sigh and slowly blink and gaze.

My bedroom window is a big one, low, with a sash, and I had been lying on my stomach doing my homework.

I had finished this now and by lying with my elbows supporting my hands which were under my chin my nose rested on the bottom of the sill. Thus above the sill were only my great glasses and my luminous and disgusting orange hair.

I am very long-sighted. I took my glasses off and gazed across the evening. There stood our garden first, pretty as a fire-screen, a lovely hazy embroidered mixture of hollyhocks, tobacco plants and roses all tangled up together against an old brick wall. Beyond the garden was the kitchen garden of the House with the Fives Court at the end of it, surrounded by tall trees, and then to my eyes more clear than all the rest was the distant high line of moors drawn with a sharp point across a great gentle sky. There were late sounds from the Fives Court, plonk, ker-plonk, thud, bump, and yells of boys' voices. Somewhere about I could hear a boy practising on a flute. One, two, three notes, pause. Yell, ker-plonk, "Oh blast you Jenks." One-two-three-four pause. Twitter of birds. The evening breeze. Ker-plonk. Onetwothreefour (go on, well done) fivesix, came the notes, then down again. Pause – then the whole phrase, effortless this time, complete. Mozart. Wonderful.

I was utterly content with the content of being in the right place at the right time. I, Marigold Green, a figure properly set in a picture, an equation on a page, a note in a bit of music, non-transposable, irreplaceable. Ugly, quaint and square lay I, happy and at home where I belonged. Sleepily and happily I watched the boy with the flute – it was nice ordinary Boakes – walk mazily through the lettuces, beneath me across the lawn.

"BILGEWATER."

I jumped so my chin cracked down on the window ledge. I swivelled my eyes, grabbed my glasses and stuck them on to my face.

"FILTHY BILGEWATER."

I turned my face and saw the boy Terrapin hanging out of a window. He was twelve then, a new boy, but he had made himself felt from the moment he had arrived last September. Even though he was quite close – the dormitory sticking out at right-angles from the Private Side and looking down at our garden too – I couldn't mistake him. He had a voice, prematurely breaking, like a rookery.

"BILGEWATER! FILTHY BILGEWATER! WATCHING US UNDRESSING!"

Then I noticed that there were other boys behind him inside the open windows, springing about getting ready for bed. Terrapin I saw had no clothes on his top half and his bottom half was hidden by the window. Behind him I could see a leaping figure now and then, very white and dazzling, swinging pairs of pyjama trousers round its head.

"BILGEWATER'S GOT A FILTHY MIND," sang Terrapin.

A hand came out of a window over his head, got down into his hair and jerked him back out of sight and the dormitory monitor looked out — Jack Rose, a year older than me — looked out quickly, rather embarrassedly, saw me, gave me a curt nod and vanished.

Jack Rose was the nicest boy in the school. There's always one, says Paula. Silver spoon boys, she calls them — good-looking, good at games, good at work and charming. Intending to be a doctor. They're always going to be doctors, Paula says. Once when he had seen me coming along home from school he had tweaked my hair as if it wasn't vile and said "Hello Marigold," (not Bilgewater) and I had dropped my satchel with the ecstasy of it all. A great huge heap of homework I'd been carrying had gone shooting over the pavement and he had helped pick it up and walked back home with me. He had pulled a funny face but not derisive at the door of the Private Side and winked. I cared more for Jack Rose's good opinion than for rubies and the sound of trumpets.

And now he believed — what did he believe? He believed I was — Whatever did he think? He thought I was a — (I began to blush scarlet) — a Peeping Tom! With the full horror of it I began to sink down on to the floor two feet beneath the sill and to press my face into the linoleum, rolling my cheeks against it, then into the smooth surface of my homework book. Perhaps I am, I thought. Perhaps I am a Peeping Tom. I began to weep. I asked to die.

I decided that if ever I have a daughter like me which heaven forbid, I shall be available on an occasion like this. I shan't be taking Private Coaching like father or out playing wild and passionate tennis like Paula. I shall be there.

"Darling — whatever's the matter? Whyever are you crying?"

"Oh, oh, he said I was a Peeping Tom."

"Don't be ridiculous, Marigold. Who said you were a Peeping Tom? What rubbish!" and my sweet mother's head shoots from the window. Glare, glare of her eyes towards the dormitories. "You boys be quiet and go to bed at once." Down comes the window.

"Marigold darling, don't cry. Don't be silly. Who said – ?"

"Terrapin said."

"Terrapin! You goose, you goose, you beautiful goose! (My what a wallow!) Will you please sit up and blow your nose and tell me whenever anybody listened to Terrapin?"

"Never." (Gulp. Sob.)

"Well then – "

"He said – "

"As if anyone would ever peep at Terrapin! At Terrapin!" Watery smile.

"They'd turn to stone. Like the Gorgon's head."

(Giggle. Laugh.)

Incident over. Terrapin ever after called the Gorgon's head and my mother and I laughing about it as the years roll by. "D'you remember that night when Terrapin called you a Peeping Tom?"

That's what will happen to my daughter, I thought. I'll see to that. Down on the floor I lay upon my silky exercise book for hours. After the first hour I thought, "I shall continue to lie here for ever. I shall lie here all night and I may die. No one will come." I wetted the exercise book with tears. I felt the tears trickle down my nose side and on to the page and the ink spread, turning my ugly writing to a fuzz.

"I will lie here till morning."

But after what seemed to be the best part of the night, in a daze I gave the most colossal sigh and heaved myself up and stretched up to shut the window. The Boys' Dormitory windows were still wide open but dark. The Fives Court was silent. In the glimmering shadowy night I heard steps below me and saw Paula and father coming slowly through the garden, Paula still in tennis clothes white among the flowers now faded into white as well. Father's voice was quiet and unperturbed and Paula laughed her loud nice laugh. They walked easily along together Paula swinging her tennis racquet about and passed out of sight. I felt a great yearning towards something or other, but slammed down my window as noisily as possible and went to bed in all my clothes.

The second incident was on a lovely day, too – in the summer

31

holidays with the House empty except for us, the big front door wide open and the sunshine pouring in. Paula was out in the raspberries. I'd asked her if she'd wanted help but she had wanted to be by herself. She sings when she's by herself, very loud and rather off-key. She knows this bothers me, try as I may not to show it, so often she goes off by herself and has a good sing when there's no one about.

If you remember I mentioned the swimming pool and how precious it is to me in the school holidays and how father would suddenly appear beside it as I was swimming and look at me simultaneously with Aeschylus, and, Aeschylus winning would wander away.

This day – the summer after the Peeping Tom affair – I had decked myself in a Japanese dressing gown I had found in one of Paula's clothes boxes. Goodness knows where it had come from but it's as well that it was there because I had been setting off down the main stairs in just my bathing dress and I am square and thick; but something made me turn back and have a burrow about. I took off my glasses and put a pair of queer old pink high-heeled shoes with pink feathers growing out of them on my bare feet, grabbed a towel and set off. In the hall sat Boakes, reading, outside father's study door so I was much relieved I had. As I passed I suppose he saw the feathers go by and looked up and said, "Hello. You swimming? Want to go a walk?" I said "No thank you Boakes," because it wouldn't be very thrilling since he would have read all the time with the end of his nose grazing the paper, and I sailed ahead to the pool. I swam about for a while and soon there was father who must have got rid of Boakes after setting him to the gate. After a few more lengths I looked up again to see that as usual he had disappeared, but that Terrapin had taken his place.

Terrapin was a local boy but a boarder. There are many fewer boarders at father's school than day boys and there is a long list of boys waiting to be boarders. Nowadays boarders, says Paula, all seem to come from broken homes or are in need of care and protection or are characters of exceptional depravity. You have to be pretty deserving to get in as a boarder from a distance, so you can imagine what sort of a hard case you have to be to get in as a boarder when you live just a few miles away, as Terrapin did.

32

Great rumours circulated about Terrapin – both parents were said to have put their heads in gas ovens, all his other relatives were alleged to have gone to Australia in a body rather than take him on. One somehow heard these things – half heard them from gossip among girls at the Comprehensive and what seeped into my ears around father's House though never a breath did I hear from father or Paula who never even hinted to anyone that they knew the slightest thing about any boy's private life.

But there was clearly something spectacularly odd about Terrapin because not only was he a boarder and local but now it appeared we'd got him in the school holidays, too. There Terrapin stood in father's place at the edge of the pool.

"Hi, Bilgewater," he said.

He had a sepulchral voice now, still hoarse and rough as when breaking. Terrapin's voice was taking its time, breaking slowly, like the dawn on a wet day. But it was a voice of great power and when he spoke his eyes stuck out and cords appeared in his neck. He grunted at intervals between statements, and simultaneously with the grunts he picked his nose. He was a very short boy with fine straight white-yellow hair which came from a central point on his skull and hung down all around with his awful face peering out of the middle. He looked like a small albino ape.

I said, "Get out," and turned on my back. Then thinking of his sticking-out eyes scanning my big hips I turned on my front again.

"Where's your father?" He was looking at me and not at my face either, with a really frightful leer and I began to kick my feet up and down tremendously sending up a wake like a battleship. I rushed down the pool at a rate of knots.

When I got to the steps at the other end he was there, squatting down at the top of them waiting for me to come up, so I spread myself out underneath him with my arms and elbows lying along the railing round the edge, and I stared into the distance.

I heard grunt, grunt up above.

He said, "You haven't half got nice arms."

I kicked off and did a thundering sprint down the pool again with my head in the water all the way, only my legs moving, with water going up fit to raise rainbows. When I got to the far end I kept my back to him and hung on to the hand-rail. When eventually I got out he had gone.

I felt sick. He was the most revolting thing I had ever seen. He was like Caliban — Paula had been reading me *The Tempest* on Thursdays — he was so foul I should have liked to get him by his beastly ankles and drag him into the water and trample him down. Every time he came up for air, all snotty, neck and eyes bulging, down I would bash him.

"Bilge! Bilgewater! Help! Help!"

"*Down* you go, you filthy boy."

"Help! Help! I can't swim!"

"Drown then!"

But the terrible thing at the time — I think I was thirteen. I might just have been fourteen. Perhaps I was twelve — the unthinkable thing was that when he said that about my arms I felt pins and needles sweep over me in a wave, starting at the top of my skull, rushing downwards to the base of my spine.

"You haven't half got nice arms."

I examined my arms that night at bedtime, turning them outwards and inwards. I have a pale skin and a very precise blue vein going diagonally across the inside of the elbow. The hands at the ends of the arms are all right, too, with pointed effective fingers and clean nails. I like clean nails.

Mrs Gathering, the headmaster's wife at father's school, once came to tea when I was small. She brought her daughter — the one I rather got on with, the one who went away. Funnily enough I can't remember the daughter on that occasion though I think there was something about her breaking one of my dolls — all I remember is Mrs Gathering getting hold of one of my hands by the tea trolley and saying "Beautiful hands". She said it dramatically. I thought she was a bit of an ass. But I remembered the compliment — my first. This one of Terrapin's was my second.

My hands and my arms. My hands and my arms. I asked Paula next day if I could have a sleeveless dress and she said "Yes my duck. If ever I get the toime."

There is one more unnerving incident. The mention of the headmaster's wife has reminded me of it. It was the summer before last when I was fifteen and took place in the lavender walk which is a sort of love-nest in the local park much patronised by my form at the Comprehensive late in the evenings. They get in over the railings by the railway bridge with father's school day-boys. It must be quite crowded in the lavender walk on moonless nights by the way they all talk about it before prayers next day while I am sitting gooping out of the window.

I love the park. It is overgrown and often empty. On weekday summer mornings to wander there is like being in a private garden. It has a high-hedged, mediaeval look. Round a corner might appear tall folk in wimples, veils and scarlet tights and shoes with curling toes, serenading each other with lutes. Down a rose garden you might glimpse a turret with a trumpeter and a fleecy cloud. I was wandering there drowsily one morning after O levels when we had time off and there was no Prep. and there was no one about to talk to at home. The smell of the lavender in the hot morning sun was enough to turn heads much more sensible than mine.

And Mrs Gathering came suddenly humping out of a lavender bush.

She said, "Marigold! Marigold!" and her big soft eyes mooned down.

"Marigold!" she said. I didn't recognise her at first – what with the house in France and in Wiltshire and a solitary nature she was a woman seldom seen about St Wilfrid's. She was given to sofas and thinking. Some people said that she suffered from melancholia, others from her husband, father's Headmaster who is a pewsy man, little and plump, like a dynamo in a dog-collar, a great writer of lists, a man of committees. He never does any actual teaching now except for a lesson or two of Theology which he never calls Scripture or R.E. or anything like that. He distributes the Theology to a very favoured few, the ones who are chosen by him for his old Oxford College. It is said that he makes a special trip to Oxford each Autumn, the season of UCCA and mellow fruitfulness. "All my boys," he says, "are sure of a Place and most of an Award." This is rubbish as father and the Thursday Club often remark – because it is years now since the school has had a scholarship to Oxbridge and even Places are getting rather few and far between. The school has been on the down with Dr Gathering. "I make a point of still knowing a *lot* of people," he says, handing all his work over to father and making for his first class carriage and the best train south. His visits co-incide with his daughter's half terms at Cheltenham. He goes on to her after Oxford – it is astonishing how she is kept out of sight – and then proceeds to his London Club.

He returns looking much rested and his wife during his absence looks much rested, too. She is even sometimes seen about the town dressed in memorable clothes of a purplish sort and not by any means warm enough for the time of the year. Sometimes she walks along the sea-front and into Boots or a flower shop. Once she was seen carrying a small sheaf of corn and an ornamental bread loaf all the way along the prom, away past the pier to the parish church which was getting ready for its harvest festival. She is rather like a harvest festival herself – an immense storehouse of a woman with a large though indeterminate face. She's like someone you've vaguely heard about in a rather bad book.

"Not at 'oame 'ere," says Paula often, "thoase Gatherin's. They're Southerners."

"Well what about you?"

"They're different. Different again from me."

"How?"

Paula thumped the iron about and turned it flat side up and gazed intently at it as if it knew the answer. The silver triangle was scorched all over with rusty stripes where she had burned things.

"You'll burn your face."

She moved the iron nearer to her cheek, country brown and red though it had seen little but cold Yorkshire weather for years.

"I don't know roightly," she said. "It's what used to be called County. Before that it was Gentry."

"Gentry's a bit ancient," I said, "and I don't like County. It's not right to say County."

"You mean it's not county to say County. Don't you come this Marxism-we're-all-one with me."

"No – I don't mean that," I said. "But it's only people who think they're less than County who talk about County. I'm not less than Mrs Gathering."

"Nobody could be *more* than Mrs Gathering." We laughed and

36

Paula put the iron down and was Mrs Gathering round the kitchen. First she was Mrs Gathering walking about and picking flowers, waving her hips extremely slowly. Then she was Mrs Gathering arranging herself on her sofa and meditating on Lovely Ideas: and then – because I may as well tell you that Paula is like this – she became Mrs Gathering in bed with Dr Gathering who was the little fat cushion Paula puts under boys' heads when they're concussed after rugger. Slowly, slowly Mrs Gathering folded Dr Gathering into her arms and moaned, "Ooooooooh! Horold!" Dr Gathering's name is Harold but Paula says that in the south and among the County that is the way it is pronounced, the letter a.

Oh Paula makes you die, and when I met Mrs Gathering soon after this in the lavender walk I had to try very hard not to remember the concussion cushion and dissolve. I blinked like mad. I wriggled about. I grinned very wide. She seemed surprised by the grin which was a very thorough-going affair for the smallness of the occasion, but she took my hand in hers and I heard her say, "Marigold. Marigold Green. Your dear mother – " and her eyes grew damp. "Such a sad shame. It might have been so different."

She was looking now of course not at my grin but at my skirt hem which was coming down and at a hole in the knee of my tights. Paula is termagantal about clean fingernails but never sees clothes. The sole of one of my sandals was flopping about a bit, too. But I was furious because all this damp-eyed business was nothing more or less than criticism of Paula and father. "I am perfectly happy," I announced, and gave her a good hard gleam from behind my specs. They are plastic non-break lenses and if you get the angle right you can magnify the eye-ball just about enough to fill the lens. It was an immature thing to do at fifteen I suppose but it was the fruit of years of practice and for some time had done rewarding things to Miss Bex my form-mistress and could sometimes make her yelp and knock jam-jars full of daffodils down the back of the bookcase, drip, drip, drip, all over the red Warwick Hamlets, making them bleed.

"Oh, of course my dear," said Mrs Gathering falling back, and I noticed for the first time (you see how big she is) that Jack Rose was standing just behind her, holding her Boots library books. She had been strolling round the park with him, father's House Captain,

Captain of Rugger, tall as a lily, all among the lavender and the red hot pokers.

And Jack had a very confident and pleased look on his face as he watched me and smiled down at me encouragingly. He had grown even more gloriously good-looking since the time he had yanked back horrible Terrapin from the window in the Peeping Tom business three years ago. He looked very strong and clean and clear-skinned – a creamy sort of complexion like a pale Spaniard. A bit like hers. His eyes were brown like hers too, but where hers were round and moist and wandering his were small and watchful. I have a thing about brown eyes. I don't mean that I dislike everyone with brown eyes but whenever I feel that I want someone to matter to me I am slightly relieved if their eyes are blue. Paula says I'd be lonely in India or Wales.

Noticing Jack Rose's eyes now was a very curious experience. I thought

1. They're brown
2. They're little
3. But it's Jack Rose. Jack *Rose*. My life and my love.

And then in a mighty rush came

4. He is in the park with Mrs Gathering and they have just come out of a lavender bush!

I have said that those two Terrapin things taught me some things about myself. I have said that all my long quiet life with only grown ups has taught me about maturity. What I discovered now was a surge of excitement and distaste and interest and misery and curiosity and a sort of envy about something in common with both. I was seeing something I didn't understand and did not want to.

No I wasn't. I was seeing something I had always understood and wanted to understand better.

What did I want to know? I looked at Jack Rose's hands, long white, medical hands, stroking Mrs Rose's library books and then, looking quickly away found myself gazing at the deep V of Mrs Gathering's lilac crêpe morning dress. Her neck down to the V was rather red and the skin thickish with minute raised pimples all over it. It was an *old* neck. I looked back at Jack Rose's unlined beautiful blank pale face high up above the pair of us. I could have wept. I don't know why.

Oh yes I do.

Chapter 4

A MOVE HAD been afoot at the Comprehensive to make me do my
A levels in one year instead of two. I had got my O levels to
everybody's surprise and had even managed to get a pass in
English, as the set book had been a very easy one, *Under the
Greenwood Tree*. I didn't particularly like *Under the Greenwood Tree*
except that it sounded like Dorset and had traces of Paula in it now
and then which made me grin, though Paula had a bit more fire
and brimstone about her. I got Paula to read me the whole book
right through one night and didn't bother with the English mistress's notes at all. In the Greenwood Tree lessons I just sat thinking
of this and that, and not feeling superior as I knew Miss Bex the
English mistress thought I was. I don't know why Miss Bex was so
sure I hated her. I wouldn't have come across a lot of things
without her.

One day for instance she read out something that was most
astonishingly interesting. It was something Hardy said about
novels. A novel, said Hardy, should say what everybody is thinking but nobody is saying.

A novel must be true.

I dare say it doesn't sound very extraordinary to most people
but it did to me. Think of it – TRUE. True like a theorem. True like
an equation. Naked and unashamed. I said it aloud, "Naked and
unashamed," I said and Miss Bex said, "Hullo? Yes? What? Was
that *Marigold*?" I couldn't think of anything else to say but I was still

so enchanted by what Hardy had said that I gave her a big grin and nodded my head, and then I sort of waved my hand at her.

She looked very uneasy and the rest of the class began to splutter and cough and make a great to-do with handkerchieves. Miss Bex said that will do now, and turned with a flurry to the board which she tapped with the chalk and I think because she was playing for time she wrote on the board: *The novel should express what everybody is thinking but nobody is saying*. Then she turned and glared at me menacingly and for a long time, even after the words had been rubbed off and covered up by Algebra next lesson — it was one of those green black boards that show through for weeks even after you've tried to get it out with water — I felt a warmth and satisfaction as I saw the words hollowly gleaming behind the symbols — facts behind facts. Truth behind truth. And on my way home the night of the Hardy lesson, as if to crown the beauty of it all by myself, I met Jack Rose. He was coming along Madeira, which is the road beside the railway line which has a rose-red wall the other side of it, the back wall of Victorian houses with long kitchen gardens, that catches any sun we get and faces south. Like the night I was a Peeping Tom, it was a balmy evening and I was sauntering along imagining myself to be Fancy Day looking at my pretty, unbespectacled face in a mirror on a cart. I was trailing my shopping basket full of books in one hand and watching the tufts of grass between the paving stones which looked like fuzzy seaweed — it's interesting sometimes to be long-sighted. And there was Jack Rose beside me.

"Hullo," he said.

He had a kind face. I mean, kind. Not soppy or twee but kind. Good-natured and loving. His hair was soft and brown and clean. He swooped and took my basket full of books from me and swung it. "Plenty of homework," he said. He had books of his own in his other hand and dropped them in my basket. His books mingled with mine. Oh God! I loved him — looking at our books together, jumbled in a heap. Then the top book fell off and I caught it and gave it back to him. It was called *Ulysses*, a huge heavy thing. "Thanks," said he, "not that I'd mind losing it too much."

"What is it? Is it Greek?"

"No. It's English. Supposed to be a novel. It's just some poor perisher's thoughts going on and on. Want to read it?"

He picked it out and solemnly presented it to me and although it was only from St Wilfrid's Library and I'd have all the trouble of getting father to take it back, I was thrilled because no one had ever given me a heavy book to read before, knowing that I found reading difficult. It was common knowledge that I could hardly read. "A present," he said bowing and I held *Ulysses* close to my heart and Rose swung along beside me talking of things like cricket and the summer holidays and all the things he was doing as if I had been anybody or attractive.

At the House Boys' Entrance we stood chatting and boys came and went between us, bursting out like rabbits free until Prep. Boakes came out and smiled at me. Then out blundered Terrapin and fell over Rose's feet. Rose kicked him. "Get up slob. You nearly knocked Bilgewater over."

"I didn't. I knocked you."

"Well, apologise."

"Not on your — ow!"

"Now get."

Terrapin rubbing a twisted arm looked at me and saw the book and read its title on my chest. "You're not reading that!" he said and started laughing.

"Get!"

Terrapin ignored him. "You won't like it, Bilge. You leave that alone."

"Why?" I was so angry I was sweaty.

"It's not fit," said Terrapin. "And you'll never get through it it's so long. And it's all boring private thoughts. It's the way you use words when you're thinking."

"I'm interested in that."

"So there you are," said Rose and (oh glory) for the second time in my life tweaked a bit of my hair. "That's what Bilge likes."

"A novel should contain what everyone is thinking and nobody dares to say," I announced and there was a bit of a pause. Jack Rose said, "So you see, Terrapin. She *has* got the right book. It's later than you think." He sort of eyed me and disappeared into the school.

Meeting Terrapin's crazy round eyes which were not kind at

42

all, I couldn't help saying that I hadn't actually started *Ulysses* yet. "I don't actually understand what its – "

"You won't at the end of it either," he said, "But I expect you'll love the bit about stuff coming out of his sister's navel." He went in through the door and then bobbed out again and his face was worse than usual – CONTUSED and ferocious.

"And there's a lovely long bit about someone pushing on the lavatory. All he's thinking about while he's – Oh dear old Thomas Hardy," he yelled, and I could hear his horrible laughing all through the garden and up our stairs and into Paula's sitting room which was empty, and the Mrs Thing of the moment had forgotten to get me any tea.

Now whether it was *Ulysses* or not – and I don't think it was because I never did get through it – Uncle Pen had got it into his head that I was dreaming about, and should have a shot at the A Levels a year early.

I had done a lot of extra work with my father in the holidays and when I took the A levels and got top grades there was a great confabulation between Pen and Puffy and father and Paula, and letters were written to Miss Bex and my Headmistress. Miss Bex who as I have said has never liked me at all asked me to stay back after school one day for a little talk and I discovered that someone – Uncle Pen again I should think – had murmured the idea that I might get in to Cambridge. Miss Bex told me of the idea as if it had been her own, offering it to me as if it had been a great big sticky chocolate. She sat back brightly to watch me lick my chops.

I examined the chocolate thoughtfully and then said I would have to take it home to father. She began to slap papers about on her desk, disappointed. She had wanted me to be excited and grateful. I couldn't see why I should be. For years and years Miss Bex, who taught English, had made me feel a fool. For years and years it had been Miss Bex who had missed me out going round the class reading because she thought I was educationally sub-normal. The A levels must have surprised her, but she had never said so – never said, "Well done".

"I think I ought to say," she called to me as I gathered my books up to set off home, "that I am *not* very confident. It seems to me to be a very – *ambitious* idea."

So it did to me. It seemed the most astounding idea. I hadn't really got used to the fact that I wasn't dim and I had never even considered any university let alone Oxbridge in my life. I suppose it is another example of my queerness that I had never thought about after school at all. If vague thoughts of it ever obtruded I had damped them down fast, with the help of the memory of Miss Bex's familiarly exasperated face.

"The General Paper would be the trouble," said father when I told him.

"Can I get help with that?" I asked. "Isn't it some sort of essay thing?"

"English," said Paula, putting down a tea tray. "Could you sign this for Boakes's boil pills, William?"

"No, no Paula. No, no."

"Why not?"

"Well the reading. The body of reading."

"She reads all right now."

"I am not deaf," I said, "I am here. I am in your presence."

"There are all the years she didn't. No, no. Too much to make up." But I could see as he pushed the signed medical form back to Paula and at her earnest look back at him that he felt excited and I suddenly saw all the anxiety they must have had about me all the long years when I couldn't tell a b from a d: the worry that there was something wrong with me. All Paula's evenings reading to me came back, and the memory of her unshakeable faith – whatever the secret notes from staff I had had to carry back from school, saying ought I not to be assessed by psychologists or the organisers of loony bins and so on – that I would be all right in the end.

I had never thought I'd have to do any English again after O level and my writing is still very bad. Also the A level English teacher is Miss Bex – need I say! – and the books she was doing with the English lot were lovely ones and I didn't want them to be spoiled. I have always preferred thinking about a book to writing about it and I have always assumed that English was the subject along with Scripture meant for the duds or those who do things just for enjoyment. But for a General Paper – ?

"Oh well," I said, "All right. I'll do some English."

"It's your decision," said father. Paula went prancing off like the triumph of Jerusalem.

Miss Bex however did not. "Really?" she said. "English? For the General Paper for Oxbridge?"

"For Cambridge."

I felt absolutely dreadful saying it. I knew I hadn't really got a hope of Cambridge although my Maths and Physics were all right.

I began to blush dreadfully and Miss Bex gave a little sardonic laugh. "Well," she said. "I suppose we might let you have a *try*. I think I had better have a word with your parents. Will you ask them to contact me?"

"It's only my father," I said. "My mother died."

"Oh. Oh. I'm so sorry. I didn't – I hope it wasn't – ?"

"Some time ago," I said bravely.

"Oh dear. Did the Headmistress – ?"

"I didn't talk about it," I said. (I couldn't have talked about it. Having just been born it was before I could talk. I am not proud of this conversation and I ought not to be pleased that she looked so terribly embarrassed.)

"I'll write to your father," she said. "Perhaps he would let me come and have a little talk with him?"

"That would be better," I said, "than his coming here. He doesn't go out of the House much. He lives a very quiet life."

She said, "Ah."

A week later I looked out of my bedroom window and sure enough there she was walking around the garden yacketing away at father, her head wagging, very earnest, and father leaning courteously towards her with his lovely absent-minded smile. As I watched he picked her a late rose – or perhaps just picked it and held it out for admiration, but she took it with great exclamations and stuck it into her big check tweed suit.

"Whoever's that?" asked Paula over my shoulder.

"That's Miss Bex. I'm doing Hamlet and Hardy with her."

"God save them," said Paula.

"Oh go on," I said, "she's clever. She knows a lot."

"She'd have to," said Paula. "I wonder what Hamlet and Hardy would have thought of *her*."

I had never heard Paula unkind like this. She's usually so un-

45

concerned about looks.

The next Monday when I met Miss Bex in a corridor she gave me a wide emphatic smile showing both rows of teeth and the little dampness that collects at each end of her mouth and causes a slight noise as she talks like a singing tap – a tap whose washer isn't quite gone but will not last much longer. Remembering Paula's unattractive attitude however, which I had found shocking, it being so very unusual, I didn't give her the basilisk lens contortion I reserve for our chance encounters.

"*There* you are," said Bex, "You'll be joining us this afternoon?"

"Will I?" I said, "What exactly – ?"

"My Wordsworth and my Hamlet class."

"Am I in it?"

"Well of course my dear. Didn't your father tell you?"

"He must have forgotten."

"*Such* a dear," she said. She could hardly be meaning me so presumably it was father. "We don't see each other all that much," I said, and then could have kicked myself seeing a wave of pity come all over her face. "*So* brave," she said, "*So* busy."

Now when I had begun to think carefully about doing extra English for the General Paper I had realised that I was glad. O level English of course is absolute rubbish – computer fodder. Kiddiwinks' crosswords – but I had enjoyed the actual books. There had been some Wordsworth. I liked him. There was a good, solemn purpose about him and I liked the way he used to pace about the Lake District making up poems with Dorothy running behind and then kindly writing them all out. The distaste that Wordsworth seemed to have had for the act of writing made me feel close to him. And I liked the way the Wordsworths wrapped themselves up in blankets out on the fells and just lay there, getting things straight as the rain poured down. And that great big unhappy nose.

And Wordsworth's passion at the glory of the lakes, shaking and shining under the rolling sky. I wondered if Wordsworth had long sight. Dorothy it seemed to me probably had short sight. Precise. I loved Dorothy. Such an awful cook. I sat thinking about her and her brother throughout the whole of the first lesson with

Miss Bex whilst the others took careful notes. Only at the end of the lesson did I decide that there must be something more to be discovered than the structure of the Wordsworths' optic nerves.

I made a conscious decision – Miss Bex I realised was speaking to me and I had just been gazing back – that I would set about this English business seriously. I would begin to work really hard – since the first bell was going – at her Hamlet class which was coming next. I said "Thank you Miss Bex," in answer to whatever she had been saying to me and also because she was looking rather exhausted and does try so, and the damp bits round her mouth were beginning to show again. "Poor Bex," I thought. "I'm going to please her. I'm going to change. I'll surprise them," and looking round I rather wished there were someone I could tell. I looked all round everyone and felt rather sad, for there were all the same old lot I'd gone up the school with, all indoctrinated with the idea that Marigold Bilgewater Green was ghastly, all in a huddle together.

For the very first time in my life I wished hard – I think perhaps I may have prayed – for a friend. I forgot Paula's Second Law. Her First Law is BEWARE OF SELF PITY but her second law runs it very close: PRAY WITH CARE. The frightening thing about prayers, she says, is that they are usually answered.

Well, off we went – there were twelve of us – into the Hamlet class. We were what was called Set B and few of us had done more than read bits out of Hamlet before. Not one of us had seen it except for a very terrible film that had been brought to the school in a bag and showed Hamlet looking pretty ancient in a gold wig wailing about some battlements in clouds of what looked like steam.

Before this lesson Bex had had them all reading round the class, but it was so dreadful that now she had us up in the front like twelve-year-olds acting it from our books. As usual there were not enough books to go round so Rosencrantz and Guildenstern were sharing and chucking the book over to the Queen when needed. Polonius was bobbing about reading over the shoulder of the First Player and I remember that a very weird girl called Penelope Dabbs was dragging herself, stomach downwards, across the floor, being Hamlet, and gazing with great intensity at the King to see if he was going to have a funny turn. Her eyes stuck out on stalks as she directed them at the King (played by Bex) and she also held the book high in the air off the floor. As chief chap she at least had been allowed a book to herself, but as she waved it around, rolled her eyes, dragged her stomach over the splinters crying out and carrying on as Hamlet does, it did occur to me as odd that this was what was necessary to get me into Cambridge.

I wasn't in it of course.

Since the time when I couldn't read I haven't been asked to take part in things and I just sat there at my desk. Outside it was raining. The classroom had grown very dark. The desks were all at untidy angles, pushed back, and the dirty blackboard behind and the awful flowers in vile vases on the ledges were especially depressing. Flowers in classrooms are as depressing as flowers in hospitals – they just emphasise the fact that you can't get out and see them growing. Classrooms break your heart.

"No!" bellowed Bex at Penelope Dabbs. "Not – oh, you are a stupid year! A *stupid* year!"

"Blaa blaa blaa," droned somebody else.

"Blaa blaa blaa," wailed forth Penelope Dabbs, and behind them all the door opened and a radiant vision appeared.

For a moment it hung on the air. The door swung slowly back and forth and then the vision was gone.

"Hullo?" called Bex, swinging round. "Did someone knock?" She looked questioningly at me as I was the only one who hadn't got her back to the door. As usual I said nothing but not for the usual reason, that no one was interested.

I gawped.

The door opened again, wider this time and a girl came in and leaned against the edge of it and leaning back began to swing herself gently to and fro. Then as if her eyelashes were too heavy for their lids she half shut her eyes and surveyed Miss Bex and everybody else from beneath them. They were great thick black eyelashes like hearth brushes and above were very beautifully marked black eyebrows which one would have expected to have been painted on and yet I felt sure were not. The slits of eyes between them were a blazing turquoise.

The girl was big and looked almost boneless. She was about seventeen, I thought, with a large pale face. She wore a green dress that clung to her all over and showed off very long, white arms. But her hair was the main astonishment. It was a huge shower, a sort of waterfall of golden – well almost golden *pink*! It was like candy floss, a gigantic cloud of light. It went on and on and up and up and out and out and it gathered all the light in the whole dreary atmosphere into itself.

There she stood, sleepily against the door, easily comfortably swinging about, with all that hair – and like the eyebrows you could tell that it was natural, you can sometimes: there was no doubt of it – all that hair burning and glowing and shining like a mediaeval heavenly host in gilt and marble. And I thought, Oh my! If Uncle Edmund Hastings-Benson could see this!

"Yes?" said Miss Bex.

The girl smiled.

"Did you want me?"

Still the girl smiled.

"Is it something to do with – " Miss Bex's voice trailed off. What could this creature be to do with? Was she Ophelia en route to the brook? Not she. Large, confident, sure the girl stood.

She said at last, "Well I just don't know. I don't know where – "

"This is the Sixth Form. A level English. Set B," Miss Bex said, sharpish.

"Well, it might – "

"Whom are you looking for? Who are you?"

"Oh I do wish I *knew*." She gave a huge sigh and looked about her and seeing me in the front row staring back she said, "Oh hullo."

"Hullo," said I.

"What is all this about?" asked Miss Bex and tapped the chalk vigorously against the wall – she's a great tapper.

"Haven't seen you for years," said the Vision. "How are you?"

"I'm all right," I heard myself say. "Come in. They're doing Hamlet."

"*Hamlet*!!" Her colossal eyes opened wide as she gazed around the floor boards and P. Dabbs on her stomach: and all of a sudden I was overcome. My decision in Wordsworth to be good and take

49

English seriously and be kind to Miss Bex vanished away. I couldn't help it. I wasn't aiming to upset them. I just sort of exploded. I made a rude, loud, tearing sound with my mouth, covered it up with my hands and made a worse one, knocked my glasses off, dropped my face against the desk and howled and howled and howled with laughter. As in five years at the Comprehensive I had hardly ever uttered a sound before and hadn't laughed like this in front of anyone except perhaps Paula in the whole of my life you can imagine the rest. Someone – good old Penelope D. – smote me on the back. Someone else moved my arms up and down as in life saving. Phyllis Thompson ran for a glass of water and Bex ordered an immediate opening of all the windows.

The Vision however simply coiled herself over two chairs and waited. "Don't worry," she called. "It's all right. She does things like this. She always was barmy. Shut up Bilgie, for Pete's sake."

"For Pete's sake," she said again stretching her legs as I gasped for air and blinked my streaming eyes. She gave a friendly nod across at Bex and turned back to me. "Don't you remember me?" she said, "I'm Grace Gathering."

"Grace Gathering," I said.

"I was your best friend when we were five. Don't you remember?"

"No," I said. Then I began to. "Grace *Gathering*," I said. "But you're the Headmaster's – You're at – You're not here!"

"I am now," said the Vision.

She looked away and so did I and so did Rosencrantz and Guildenstern and Polonius and all the royal family because the background music of vehement tapping had begun to gather speed and force. Bex in her might was entrenched behind her tall desk and the chalk clattered like a gun. "Might I just be *informed*," she said, icicles forming on every fang, hoar frost puffing at the nostrils, "Might I just be *granted* – "

"Oh – I'm terribly sorry." Grace leapt up and went over to her. "I think I'm probably going to be in this form. There's no one in the staffroom or the headmistress's little nest. I suppose I was a bit late. I just thought I'd try a few doors."

"You mean," said Bex coldly, "that you are a New Girl?"

50

"Yes."

"In my Sixth?"

"I think so. I've been at a boarding school till now. I suppose I'm this sort of age." She wafted her hand about in our direction.

"I see. From which school?"

"Dartington Hall."

"I see."

"I thought you were at Cheltenham," I said and everyone looked at me as if a waxwork had uttered.

"Sacked," said Grace Gathering.

"And Dartington?" asked Miss Bex.

"Sacked too."

She gave Bex and everybody a lovely smile.

"So I've come home to mum," she said. "To School House over the road from old Bilgewater." She gave Bex an encouraging nod. "I'm sure things are going to be a lot better now."

The bell went then and somehow we got the Shakespeares gathered up and old Bex out of the room and everyone drew close together like a pondering army. They huddled, every one of them over in a group under the Watts portrait of The Man who had Great Possessions, looking as if he's being sick in a corner. Somebody knocked over a vase of the dead chrysanthemums and as the water trickled down I realised why I was feeling so good. For the group in the huddle was looking across not only at the Vision but at me, too. The Vision and I were together. We were allies!

"Chrysanthemums," said Grace smiling across at them as the water dripped, arranging herself on my desk. "Have you noticed how they look like sheep's bottoms?"

She twirled one. "In the wind," she said. "We drove over the moors from York here yesterday — all the poor sheep with their bottoms turned into the wind. Just like grey chrysanthemums."

The Bex VI, Set B, had no views on this so Grace turned back to me and tossed her pink candy floss about which did not look like dead chrysanthemums or sheep's bottoms. "Well old Marigold Bilgewater Green," she said, "it's nice to see you again after all these years. I like your hair. It's gone quite curly. It's great to see a face you know.'

Chapter 5

I WENT BURSTING home from school to Paula that afternoon as I have never done before or since, up to the ironing room, over to the sick room, the San, down to father's study and at length ran her to earth with father over in the Long Dormitory. Boys scuttered out round my feet like rats from a barn as I flew in. I banged into Boakes with his face in a book as he walked out and I collapsed up to Paula who was demonstrating blind cords and neither she nor father showed any great interest in the news I brought.

"Grace Gathering's arrived," I declared.

"Think they'd all been trying to hang theirzelves," said Paula. "Shredded to bits so they won't pull downwards, or *elze* they get pulled about too hard and ping back!"

"Ping back," said father meditatively, squinting out at a vista, "Hullo Marigold. Lovely cloud formation. Look."

"So they'll have to be renewed and it'll cost a hundred pounds and will have to be faced."

"Grace Gathering's here."

"It's not dezent the way they spring about naked." (She pronounced it to rhyme with baked.)

"Oh come now," said father, "I'm sure it's not important. Who's arrived, Marigold?"

"Grace Gathering. She's been expelled from Dartington Hall. She's coming to our school. She's going to live at home over at the Head's."

"Oh good. She'll be a friend for you," Paula said, "and I'm not having those great hairy seniors prancing about no blinds drawn and young girls about corruptible. Who's this Grace Gatherin' then?"

"Well she's Grace *Gathering*. She was once my best friend. Don't you remember. She's *terribly* friendly and she's grown simply beautiful. And *kind*," I added coldly as Paula started leaning about with a tape measure.

"What's the matter with you?" she said. "Who's *un*kind? BEWARE OF SELF PITY. All I have to get straight at the moment is whether I can order new *bloinds*."

"Couldn't you – run up some of those nice net curtains we used to have long ago?" father asked a bit exhaustedly.

"Dirt catchers. Fol-de-rols. Burned them all long since and there'll be no more in my time. After my time may be. And they need good thick bloinds in winter as well as curtains. For warmth. No patience with this Tom Brown's Schooldays fiddle-de-dee –" On and on they went.

"I'm going now," I said and they paid no attention. "I'm going across to the Head's to look her up." This was a very extraordinary thing for me to do as I never stirred foot after school over the House doorstep but all Paula cried was, "Supper. Don't forget your supper. Eggs and beans gets leathery."

"I shall be *out* to supper," I declared and vanished round the woodsheds, loitering over the road, past the other Houses, and out of sight towards the Headmaster's wrought-iron work and Georgian front door. What I thought I was going to do when I got there I know not, but the arrival of Grace had shaken me very oddly. I had felt quite certain from the moment she appeared that she had been in some way Sent – that she was some sort of salvation, even though until the moment she had put her head round the door I had not realised that I was in need of any salvation at all. Like the man who had had great possessions, I had been fine – or so I thought. I hadn't known how much I needed a friend.

A narrative and an equation are one, in that they are some sort of an attempt at a statement of truth, at what – as Hardy says – every one is thinking and nobody dares to say: so that in case you are thinking that I was a bit weird in my feelings for Grace

Gathering, a bit steamed up like the third form girls get about mistresses or Puffy Coleman gets about the new boys – let me tell you quite coolly that I am not like that. I have a very good balance of hormones all distributed in the right places. The only thing that ever worried me was that I started brewing them so early and at – well I'd better admit it – even eleven, I couldn't sometimes sleep for thoughts of Jack Rose.

But I'm not funny. My wonder and delight at the sight of Grace, at Grace's attention and friendliness to me were simply that I saw a wondrous hope in them that I might bask in them a little, might tag along. I might be associated. Something very promising had walked into Miss Bex's Hamlet with Grace Gathering – a sort of hazy hopefulness, a sleepy, delicious content of the kind I had felt that evening long ago when Boakes had played the flute by the Fives Court, or that other afternoon when I had been walking along Madeira and Jack Rose had come along and said I could read *Ulysses*.

In other words I saw that where Grace Gathering went there would be romance and that if I hung about perhaps some of it would come off on me. Romance I saw in its best Tennysonian or mediaeval sense. If a cynic of course like Terrapin were to read this he would say, "Ha – Bilge thought that Grace would attract boys and if she hung around she, Bilge, might get some of the left-overs."

But Terrapin held no threat for me. He was my evil genius of long ago. I hardly saw him now. The only two romantic episodes of my life he had squashed flat but there was no way he was going to get at this one. Grace would not even be aware of the Terrapins of this world, just as she would not be at risk from or aware of the romantic twaddle of dear old Uncle Edmund Hastings-Benson. Grace I saw as a figure far, far above coarseness or sloppiness – a figure of real Romance, a creature of turrets, moats and lonely vigils, gauntlets and chargers, long fields of barley and of rye.

And now I was to be associated with her. I imagined myself as I wandered over father's House playing fields towards the cricket pavilion then back again along the road, past Grace's house but not looking at it, back to my own home again, trailing a hand along the School House railings: I saw Grace Gathering in a floating dress and a tall cone of a hat with a flimsy bit of net fluttering behind it, drifting down to a river and lying flat out in a boat and the boat floating smooth, smooth, down the river into a pearly haze beneath bridges. And I heard Grace's voice singing, singing, softer, softer and stopping, and then at the last bridge Lancelot himself leaning sadly over, sadly gazing.

He said, "She had a lovely face
          The Lady of Shalott."

And beside him on the bridge stood I – Bilgewater. It was to me he said it.

"Alas," he said, "Grace Gathering. Dead, poor thing and not for me. Not *really* my sort of course," he said – Jack Lancelot. "Not a girl one could *really* love, really get close to," and he held out his pale doctor's hand inside its mediaeval knitted-metal glove, Jack Rose did, and lifted my hand to his lips. "Oh Bilgewater! Marigold!"

Together we walked off the bridge, together for ever with Grace Gathering's great big white and gold body sloshing about under the bridge and tipping about on the tide.

A narrative must be what everyone is thinking and nobody dares to say. I present you therefore with my obedience to Thomas Hardy, my attempt at naked truth, the thoughts I really thought, the fantasy I really had.

Though it's not somehow as good as *Ulysses*.

Chapter 6

THE NEXT DAY brought no sign of her. She didn't appear in our class and I didn't see her in prayers. "Whatever happened to that *girl*?" Penelope Dabbs sniggered. "Was she an illusion?"

"Perhaps," said Phyllis Thompson with a meaning look. She's full of meaning looks. Though nobody understands the meaning which is bad luck on her. "She's something to do with Marigold." (I'm usually Marigold at my own school if I'm anything unless they have a brother at St Wilfrid's and know.) "Who is she, Marigold?"

"She's the Headmaster's daughter. I knew her when I was little for a bit."

"She's rather weird," said Phyllis Thompson.

"She's rather much," said someone else, "she talks class."

"Clarss," said Penelope. "Where's she been all these years?"

"Being kept out of the way of the likes of us," said Doris Nattress, "in case she gets talking North."

"She'd talk how she wanted, that one," said Phyllis, "wherever she was. She'd do what she wanted."

For a moment everyone was united with envy.

"Maybe she's been in prison somewhere."

"She's not old enough."

Everyone shrieked. "Her hair's too long."

"But Dartington is a prison, isn't it?"

"No it isn't. That's Dartmoor. Dartington's a posh school

where they do as they like. They're all wicked and then they turn out terribly well in the end."

"Sounds like Enid Blyton."

They howled and screamed with mirth. I was unamused.

Wednesday came, Thursday. Then Thursday evening I was up with Paula as usual and Paula's telephone cleared its throat and she picked it up. "She's eating her supper," she said. Then, "Oh, all right then." She put the phone down and seized my plate and ran with it to the oven. "Message," she said, "You're to go and take it down there. Go on quick. They're hanging on on your father's phone."

I went off to the study, waded through everyone's outstretched feet, blinked my way through the pipe smoke to the desk where the phone was off the hook waiting for me.

"Hullo?"

"Marigold?"

"Yes."

"My *dear*. It's Girlie Gethrun heah. Yes. Girlie, Grace's mother. Isn't it lovely? She's heah! Coming to your school next week. Such fun! Much beh then bah school. Your fah *so* Sensble. Mech mah sef-raant."

"Who is it?" asked Uncle HB.

"Some mad woman," I said.

"—— so abah six-thirty then?"

"What? Sorry?" (Puffy and Old Price had got started on zeppelins close to my right ear.)

"Will six-thirty be all right?"

"All — ? Oh, yes," I said, "Lovely."

The line clicked off. "Oh heavens," I said, "I'm in a mess now."

"Nonsense, nonsense," said father gently dusting a wine glass with an antimacassar.

"But I am," I said, "I've been asked to something at six-thirty but I don't know what or which day or where."

"Ah," said father. He paused near the chess set and put down the wine glass. I drifted up. Time passed. Father moved a rook and looked at us all with a face of beatific joy.

"Aha, aha," said father — and I do not wonder, for he had set down the rook. It was the most brilliant move. It was one of the cleverest things he had ever done. It was a game that had been concerning both of us for several weeks and a sticky game up to now. With sheer admiration I sank down and found myself on Puffy Coleman's knee. He brushed me off as if I were a spider and looked huffy. Huffy Puffy.

"Cor luv a duck," I said to father, "you're a blummin' genius!" (I talked North.)

"William," said HB, "I wish you'd stop this."

"Hmmm?" said father.

"This vulgarity. Bilge's vulgarity."

"I'm *not* vulgar."

"My dear child, you are now and then. *Very* vulgar. As an old friend, a *privileged* friend who has known you since you were —"

"Hey!" I said, picking up a horse.

"—— she would not have cared for it."

"Who wouldn't?" said father, blinking.

"Daisy," said HB, meaning mother and dropping his eyes. "Daisy would not have cared for Bilge saying 'blummin' genius'."

"No," said father, slowly watching the squares. My hand hovered, my hand rose, my hand slowly fell. I donked down the horse and we both sat still for a very long time. Only Old Price's dead-leaf voice whispered on. Then the air grew electric and my father cried, "My word! My word though! Ha Ha!"

"Ha ha," he cried and he got up and came over to me and sort of biffed me over the back, "but bless me, Edmund if she's not one. *She's* the blummin' genius! My goodness gracious me!"

I had done something pretty nice. The game was far from over but what I'd done was pretty nice. I don't suppose I will ever make a better move than I made that evening. I wagged my head about and grinned at everyone. So did father. We were well pleased with each other.

"Can't get the hang of chess," said Puffy.

"Where's the wine gone?" asked HB and father began looking about for the corkscrew.

Paula had gone off to some crisis in the dormitories when I got back and I took my dinner out of the oven which had been on at number 10 by the look of the pork chop, and I sat very happy thinking of the rook and the horse. Looking back I realise that I was feeling happier than I had been since Grace had appeared. Also perhaps it was the first time I had really stopped thinking about her. Or perhaps I had not *thought*, not *thought* at all about anything since Monday, only felt; and the bit of thought or what Paula calls headwork that had occurred down in the study had restored me to myself again or at least to some sort of inner self-respect.

Difficult.

Gnawing the chop bone I thought of the rook. I thought of the mess and the muddle in father's study and the order and truth that nevertheless emerged from it. I reflected on my father's character, his vague face that hides a multitude of virtues.

Paula came in, red as a fox, red as a rose, wild as a foxglove and I smiled at her over the chop.

"There now," she cried, "So there we are! Bloind down. On his head. Concussed."

"Who?"

"Terrapin of course, who else? Poor Jack Rose tried to field it off him and puts his head right through the window. Boakes was there thank God. Tourniquet. Saved the day! Might have been the main artery."

"In his head?"

"I told you. You were *witness*. I told your father. Those bloinds. Last week. You heard me tell your father." She was running about for Elastoplast and Savlon, then to the phone for the doctor.

"Life's difficult," I said, feeling still that it was getting better really.

"Beware of self pity. You have to expect difficulties. Is that the doctor? Expect it, I say and it'll be all right. Hello? Well you'd better get over here quick-as-whats-thiz for there's disaster!"

The astounding thing about Paula is that she looks like Tess of the D'Urbervilles and she sounds like Tess of the D'Urbervilles and she thinks like Tess of the D'Urbervilles and yet she's so different from Tess of the D'Urbervilles. I expect she comes from a different part of Dorset. Life is awful for her all right, fate and doom are in control, yet she's all for doing something about it — not praying or accepting. Doing. You wouldn't catch Paula lying down on Stonehenge and waiting for the police. She'd be getting down to the headwork, packing suitcases, buying a single ticket into the heart of the madding crowd.

"Is this world a *blighted* star?"

"It is so. Now then let's see about new bloinds."

"Fool Terrapin," I said, "Brave Jack Rose."

And in this tremendous activity of the evening I clean forgot the telephone call.

Chapter 7

GRACE GATHERING was there at school all right on the following Monday. She was the first thing to be seen in prayers. The great gold head towered above the wide sea of ordinary heads some rows in front of me. It was, I saw, in a row of fifth formers. She must have been put down in the O level lot. Funny not to have got O levels at that age but perhaps she was younger than she seemed.

There were a few other large, older girls in that form as it happened and Grace Gathering was standing beside a curvaceous brown-skinned one called Beryl Something who had a bad reputation and didn't do much in the way of washing. She had long slit eyes. The distinguishing feature of Beryl Something was that for more years than you could count, probably from the moment she had arrived at the school there had been boys on motor bikes hanging round the school gates to take her home.

On the other side of Grace there was another girl I couldn't stand either called Aileen Sykes. "Aileen" just suited her. Fancy a parent choosing Aileen when there was no law against Eileen! Most names ending in leen are pretty (not Maureen or Doreen) but *Ail*een! She had a terribly old, wizened face and was undersized, neatly proportioned and dimity and terribly self-possessed. Ten times an hour she would yawn and look out of the window as if everything were too much for her. To look at her you would think that the minute she was out of school she passed into a sort of boudoir existence of levées and minuets and dishes of tay and a bit of fingering on the harpsichord. I don't think she can have done really as she lived in Pearson Street where all our Mrs Things came from and one of our Mrs Things had known her mother and said there were blacklocks in the Sykses' cake tins. There was the odd motor bike at the gate for Aileen Sykes too, and sometimes quite a cluster of quite presentable objêts d'art astride them. Aileen spoke authoritatively about the lavender walk in the park and the phases of the moon. One Thursday evening I heard dear Uncle HB say "Who is Aileen Sykes?" and I thought, Oh heavens no! Not *her* now! but it turned out that someone in his extra English set had carved AILEEN SYKES an inch deep in a new teak desk and filled it up with indelible ink. "Quite a sensible sort of feller usually, too."

Grace stood between these sirens and I watched what happened all around. Nudging, whispering, "Hey – there she is. That girl last week in Hamlet," etc. I thought, goodness, I'd better tell her to keep away from those two. She'll get a terrible reputation, and as we all began to file out after the notices I tried to catch her eye. Her form filed past before mine and had to pass the end of the row where I was standing.

She looked at me. She had a sleepy, cat-like half smile on her face. She stared right through me and drifted on.

Funny I thought.

At Break I went looking for her.

"Hullo," I said. She was with the other two and had taken some finding. It was past the end of the lovely warm summer but there was still a second crop of hay on the playing fields scratched up into mounds along the far end of them. The playing fields ended in cliff, and the haycocks were outlined against the sky, a cold, windy place, extremely dangerous and there must have been more hockey balls than stones rotting away on the sands below. To keep depressives and the victims of Miss Bex's sense of humour from leaping over the haycocks into space there was a droop of wire nailed to a few posts before you actually reached the edge. The haycocks were in front of it and it was from between the haycocks and the wire that I heard laughing as I trailed about the field as a last resort, looking for Grace.

"Hullo," I said.

Grace, Beryl and Aileen were reclining about behind the hay smoking cigarettes. Grace was painting her fingernails and the three figures looked very much at home, like old marbles on a mountain, Grace particularly though she can't have seen the place in her life before that morning. Perhaps because of the meagre amount of hay or the very narrow slip of cliff-top she looked gigantic, titanic. Big dirty brown Beryl looked impressive, too and Aileen, less abandoned had arranged herself to best advantage, cross-legged with a twirling toe. She was tapping ash and as usual yawning but the yawn when she saw me appearing round the haycock turned into a sort of disgusted grimace.

"What on earth are *you* doing?"

"Good heavens!" said Beryl and began to laugh. Although they are in a lower form they are as I say old – perhaps even eighteen – and have always found me noxiously beneath them. What I think of them has never been made manifest because I have always tried to keep the same blank, dotty expression on my face for everyone. Being thought dippy until I came out top in the A levels had been muddling for people, and it was an idea that died hard. "Well she's *academic*," they said. There was a fashion at the time for people being "not academic". "Very clever you know, but not *academic*." I was academic – but barmy just the same.

"Whatever do *you* want?"

"I came out to have a word with Grace."

"With *Grace*!"

"Yes. I wanted to see her."

Grace carefully painted a little fingernail, smiling at it.

"Well, here she is," Beryl laughed and leaned on Grace with a languid shove. They all went off into hysterics.

"Watch out," said Grace, "I've smudged it."

"You can't wear nail varnish at school," I said and heard my voice sounding just like Bex.

"My, my," said Aileen.

"Well come on then," said smelly Beryl, "let's hear what you've got to say."

"Nothing," I said. "Well, just to see how she's getting on."

I noticed that we were all talking about Grace as if she were a queen of some sort, someone you couldn't speak to direct.

"*Really!*" they said. They were nearly weeping with laughter. I suppose I was looking worse than usual. I was wearing tennis ankle socks and sort of slippers as I hadn't been able to find any tights that morning, Paula being too busy with both Terrapin and Rose in the sick room to bother about my clothes. Jack Rose's parents were never off the phone about the severed artery in his head. My new winter gym slip was about seven sizes too big for me, too, and I'd dropped my glasses that morning and one of the joints was all done up with a clutch of Elastoplast. The glasses seemed to have grown loose all over as a result and kept sliding down my nose.

"I think she fancies you," said Beryl. "She's a bit foony."

"Like her uncle Puffy Coleman," squeaked Aileen.

"Or her uncle Hastings-Benson. Bendson. Nobody's safe with him."

Beryl tittered and Grace extended her hand over the cliff edge after screwing the brush slowly into the nail-varnish bottle. She held the hand to dry above the creeping sea.

"Don't step back," said Aileen.

I didn't. But I went away.

Yet to my surprise as I got off the bus and began to walk home along Madeira, Grace was standing waiting for me, swinging a sort of knitted orange bag — a lovely one. She had a lovely orange scarf on, too. Like a dog I found myself trotting up.

She was alone and as I drew alongside she turned away and began to saunter along ahead of me without a word. "Hullo," I said jogging up. "How are you?" I couldn't believe in my voice. Awful. Ingratiating.

Then I saw Jack Rose just ahead of us. He seemed remarkably recovered though his hand (not head!) was all done up in bandages and a sling. "Oh, Rose!" I called and then cursed myself. I don't seem to be able to get anything right. Boys hate being called by their surnames unless by masters or masters' wives and then not often. A girl doing it is just the end. It is hard for me to remember this though, because at home in the House with Paula and father it's surnames for boys all the time. I didn't even know for instance what Terrapin's first name *was* though no more I suspect did even father. Terrapin was just Terrapin to everyone. Perhaps for all I knew he was Terra Pin. Or Terry Pin. But no he wasn't. I felt sure. He was Terrapin full stop. Rather like a lord. I thought, (ridiculous) Melbourne, Salisbury, El Cid. Or a clown, I thought, Grock, Cantinflas, "Terrapin": and I saw a vision before me of Terrapin's head upon the air, his round brilliant eyes, his long old face, his peculiar yellow hair. Yes, a clown.

We came up to Jack Rose at whom I had yelled "Rose" committing idiocy number one and having yelled, committed idiocies number two and three and I had (2) sounded vulgar as Uncle HB had said, and (3) had shown off to Grace that I was on yelling terms with The Most Desirable Boy at our Fathers' School. And there were no flies on Grace – she knew exactly what I had been up to. The very blankness of her face showed that she knew that I knew that she knew that I was proud of knowing Jack Rose. It also showed me quite decisively that she knew that I knew that she knew that Jack Rose was the Most Desirable Boy in the School and that she was quite unmoved by it.

Jack Rose stopped and waited and we came up with him, and, adding idiocy to idiocy I did it again. "Oh Rose," I said again with a dreadful smirk at the bandages, "thou art sick." Paula had read it to me years ago. Blake. "Oh Rose thou art sick." I hadn't understood it at all.

"Hullo Marigold," he said and looked carefully at Grace, "Hullo Grace."

"D'you know her?" I asked, surprised.

"Yes, we've met." The two of them half looked at each other. "And how are you poor Marigold Bilgewater with your glasses all awry?" He plunged into the dear-old-elder-brother act with me, towering high above my head, not taking a blind bit of notice of Grace.

"'Bye," she said with a flouncing shoulder, disappearing through her father's wrought-iron gates all hung with shields.

"What a gigantic great creature," said Rose.

"She's terribly romantic-looking though," I said. "Sort of pre-Raphaelite, don't you think?"

"How old are you, Bilgie?"

"Seventeen. Why?"

"Sometimes you seem seven."

I dashed off towards home and my glasses steamed over and I fell over my feet. I made for the first door I could – I don't know which. It might have led anywhere. In my father's House are many mansions. I was beyond caring – but Jack Rose came up behind me and spun me round, "Hey," he said. "Let me finish. Sometimes you seem seven and sometimes you seem twenty-seven. Listen. D'you know my mother?"

"Know your *mother*?"

"Yes. She knows you. She's seen you at Sports Days and things for ages. She knew yours a bit apparently. They were at school together or something."

"I don't know her."

"Well she wants you to. She's written to your father. D'you think you could just get him to answer?"

"He hasn't told me. I expect it's got a bit buried. He's just a bit – well, vaguish – "

"Yes."

"I'll try and find it."

"It's just about you coming over."

I stood in a lump.

"She rather wants you to come over. To us. At half term. Would you come? It's only three days."

"I don't know where it is." I could feel myself turning from head to foot a fiery, beating, blood-red.

"It's in the country. Well nearly. The far side of Middlesbrough. You could travel with me. Would you come?"

"Yes," I said, "All right." I staggered away and got myself into the boys' underground changing rooms, heaven knows how. There is no mansion in my father's House or any other where I would less choose to be. There were empty rows and rows of pegs, rows and rows of crumpled whitish garments, a few gym shoes, like dead fish, awash among puddles from the odd overflow tap, the smell of boy and disinfectant, all windows shut against the golden autumn afternoon – too cool for cricket, too hot for rugger where everybody must nevertheless be for the rooms were empty.

"I have been invited to stay with Jack Rose," I informed the latrines. "I have been invited beneath the very nose of Grace Gathering, the most marvellous-looking girl there's ever been in

66

this town and whom he ABSOLUTELY IGNORED."

I walked up the back stairs and came out in the boys' common room and had a moment of terror in case Jack Rose should be there again and think that I was following him. But only Terrapin was there, off games because of the alleged concussion, over in the far corner. He was shredding a blind cord and the sun shone in on his long fingers. He has beautiful hands, Terrapin.

And I did the most inexplicable thing. I walked all the way across the huge common room and sat down with Terrapin and watched his lovely clown's hands moving about. He didn't look at me. I said, "I'm going to stay with Jack Rose," and took my broken glasses off.

"For half term," I said.

He stopped shredding and looked at me.

"His mother's asked me," I said. "She was a friend of my mother. Well – it will be nice to stay in a country house."

Terrapin looked out of the window.

"They're pretty grand the Roses aren't they?" I said, "Such a bore." (And I think I may have yawned like Aileen Sykes.) "It'll mean new clothes."

He answered not a word.

And I had such a longing – so queer. I wanted suddenly to take Terrapin in my arms. There was something in his funny face, his ancient sorrowful look – I even put out my hand a little way and then I thought, "But it's Terrapin" and got up and got myself out and walked back through the changing rooms and through the garden. I passed the common room again from outside and saw his thoughtful face and the decimated blind cord hanging limply on the evening air.

Chapter 8

"So you've really done it now you soft tweddle!"

Paula stood at the top of the stairs as I reached home and she looked wild.

"What have I done?"

I thought, Oh the fuss! Whatever is it now?

"You've not deigned to turn up at a party. Not *deigned*!"

"Me?" I said, "Who'd ask me to a party? I've never been to a party since I was five."

There's a mirror in the hall and I caught sight of myself in it as I turned to shut the door. The hall door has old red and blue glass in it and was shining on me. I put my specs back on and gooped in the mirror. I looked like a bilious owl, in a violent sunset after the explosion of the final bomb. Who'd want me at a party? I pulled a face at my face and a waft of autumn breeze round the door made the mirror tap tap like a troubled heart about to have a stroke. "The mirror CRACKED from side to side," I cried and pulled a worse face.

"Now look you 'ere," said Paula advancing down the stairs. "Jes' you koindly let me know how ould you are?"

"Funny," I said, "That's the second time I've been asked that this afternoon."

"*And* I'm not surprised. I'm getting tired of you Marigold Green scumfishing about this world, scatty as Him. There's shoes and toights and dear-knows about the landing. And whatever

68

clothes you went to school in – Dear Lord in Murzy! (She had seen my nether regions) Where did you get them zockz? I put them in the Oxfam in 1970."

"There's someone been a long time with cold feet then," I said, rudely I suppose. Oh how she fumes! "Poor old things. Sitting there in the desert without any ankle socks. And starving too."

"Now then," said Paula with a snort which would have been a laugh in other circumstances. "Let's just forget Oxfam shall we? And ankle zockz shall we? And hear about Mrs Gathering's sherry party at six-thirty last Saturday evening?"

"Oh."

"Yes."

"I forgot. Well I never really knew."

"What do you mean – never really knew? She telephoned Thursday – says you accepted. She didn't ask your father but *you*, personally (burzonally) on account of this Grace. You said you'd be there."

"Oh heck."

"And that'll do swearing."

"Oh Paula. I did forget. I utterly forgot. It was the chess. Oh heavens. That's why she's gone so nasty – Grace. What shall I do?"

"You'll apologoize. At once."

"Oh help – I couldn't."

"You'll bath. You'll remove they zockz and shoes, you'll put on your brown and you'll eat your tea. Then across the road to that Gatherin's front door and apologoize."

"Couldn't I write? Or ring up. And talking of age, Paula, I *am* seventeen. It's my affair."

"You don't know 'em. You don't know 'em well enough for telephones. You go in humble apology. Dear Lord!"

"Perhaps I'd better go to the back door. Perhaps I'd better put no shoes on and go bare foot. Perhaps you could kindly get me some fire ash to scatter in my hair."

"Now don't you shout at me. You'll disturb your father." She was away twirling taps in the bathroom, scattering bathsalts in volcanoes of steam. I hadn't a hope.

And whatever was I going to say, anyway? In the brown suit

with the padded shoulders and box pleats which had been Paula's and had still, so she said, some years of wear in it, and a hat she'd bought me last year in Binns's sale (felt, with a brim and a little bird's feather) I set forth across the road, through the great gates and across the noisy gravel. "I ought to be doing some work," I grumbled and lifted the great knocker. "If I'm really supposed to be trying for Oxbridge."

The School House is the best bit of architecture in the town. It is eighteenth century and benign and it has all the original eighteenth century glass in the windows which gives it (Boakes once told me – he's mad on this sort of thing) a particular light. There is a fluted fanlight over the door and lovely curving steps leading up to it.

Donk went the knocker.

What could I say? I had work to do. Why was I wasting time here? "I'm terribly sorry that I forgot – " "I am Marigold Green from Green's House. Please could I speak to Mrs Gathering." "I'm so terribly sorry –"

Who would come to the door? Perhaps Grace. She'd say, "Oh you again. Are you following me around or something?" What if the Headmaster came to the door himself? He didn't know me from Adam. He'd think I was selling things. What if Jack Rose came to the door?

This idea filled me with such horror – it shows what a state I was in – that I began to shake. If I'd thought about it I am sure I would have seen how unlikely it was. Jack Rose is in father's House, even though he's head boy of the whole school and Dr Gathering thinks he's the Angel Gabriel. He wouldn't be over in the school house now. He'd be taking Prep. at home or resting his bad arm in his study or talking to father. What made me think he was here?

Yet I was so sure that he was here that I almost saw the door open and his dignified face come round it. "Oh – Bilgewater again! Are you following me about?"

I began to blush and tremble and turned away and set off back down the gravel before I realised that I had been wasting all this misery on a completely hypothetical situation for in fact nobody was going to open the door at all. My donk had not been heard. I was a little off my head. Academic but barmy.

Then as I turned away and made off the door did open. I heard it

70

behind me, and running feet and Uncle Edmund HB went tearing past me wild of eye and dragging his shooting stick. He passed me, reached the noble gateway, slithered to a stop, slewed round and said, "Oh. Yes. Ha." There was an all-too-familiar light in his eye.

"Ha. Bilge. Have you seen your father?"

"No. He'll be coaching."

"Long?"

"Oh yes – hours on Mondays."

"Must have a word. Are you coming or going?"

I tried to remember. Looking back at the door which he had left wide open I saw someone cross the hall inside and my heart sank. There was someone in and I would have to try again.

"Well going. Going in there. I have to."

"Ah. Aha. Calling on the new friend?" He turned salmon pink. "Grace?" he breathed.

"No. Mrs," I said sternly and turned back.

There are times when my environment appears to me as very much less than educative and the rational element in man to be so miniscule that you wonder what creation is all about and turn to chess or cats or mathematics as to straws upon the sea.

The idiocy of it. Uncle Hastings B. rising eighty. I, Bilgewater, rising seventeen, and he ready to reveal to anyone, in a moment even to me, the flutterings of his worn old heart over a girl of my own age – ready to discuss such things with me as if I were a comrade of the Somme. How old are you? How old are you? How old are you? Oh Bilgewater. Oh Uncle Pen how old are you?

I began to reflect on the nature of experience and particularly of experience not advancing maturity. Experience. Experio. Experire. So many levels encompassing one definition. $x = a + b + c + d + e + f + g + h + i + j + k + l + m + n + o + p + q + r + s + t + u + v + w + x + y + z$: but yet possibly equalling only some of these or different combinations of them. But x can also = o. Can some people experience and remain unchanged?

No.

Experire.

In the nature of the word –

But some people can experience, and retain innocence. Some people can experience on a queer, shallow level in order only to recount. For some, experience is only a vehicle, a pipe, a jug. Experience to such people is given only to be handed on. The creative artist I supposed was such a person, seeing, stretching for pen or brush or MS paper or a stage, shouting, "Here is my experience, COMPREHEND", and having shouted forgetting and surviving.

But Uncle HB — he'll never be all right. This agony and unfulfilment, each time exactly as before. Woman after woman after woman. My mother down to Mrs Bellchamber and now Grace. Next — someone else no doubt. What, will the line stretch to the crack of doom?

And I, Bilgewater. I seem to experience and experience, I thought. On I go, experiencing. I ought to be quite worn out. Yet I don't seem to change either. I don't seem to get wiser or find anything easier.

"I don't feel any better at all," I said to myself looking down at Paula's brown herringbone tweed and a queer pair of blue high-heeled shoes I'd found under the stairs. Under the shoes there seemed to be grass which was odd as a moment before there had been gravel. Looking to left and right of the shoes there was a lot more of it, with some white metal hoops about. Whatever — oh my goodness! I looked up and behind me and, yes, it was true! I was on the Headmaster's lawn at the back of the School House. The door behind me was a garden door and led back into a hall and at the end of it I could see the back of the front door open on to the front drive. While I had been considering the elements of experience I had walked right through the Gatherings' house and out into their garden.

What was worse, there on the croquet lawn, at some little distance were some graceful, laughing people. They were moving over the lawn towards me in a way that was confident and amused and which scared me to death. They came on. They swung mallets, one wore a great romantic hat. They moved easily inside their clothes, cheerful, languid.

Experienced.

Older than me, younger than Hastings-Benson, but filled with blessed self-respect. On they came, four or five of them across the lawn, laughing like what Paula calls County, smiling, enjoying themselves.

Water-snakes, I suddenly thought. Like Coleridge's water-snakes. "Slimy things that crawled with legs" – but phosphorescent, adapted, cheerful. I envied them. "I blessed them unaware." They scared me stiff but I blessed them unaware.

"And who is this?" asked water-snake one (The Headmaster), mellifluous and kind.

"Why, *Marigold*," said water-snake two (Mrs Gathering) and I took to my awful high heels and fled.

Chapter 9

"THERE'S A VISITOR for you. Come on now."

Paula's voice through the door was quieter, more bewildered than usual. I had come back the night before, running, running through the garden, dashed past her and father in the hall and up-stairs into my bedroom. There I had locked the door, drawn the curtains and flung myself on the bed. Much later when the various rantings and ravings and bangings on the landing had stopped I had got out of bed, taken all my clothes off and bundled them in a heap in the grate, pulled on my striped pyjamas, got into bed, covered my head and lay like a carcass under the blankets through the hot, late evening.

Clinking of a supper tray left cunningly on the landing, even a tactful cough and "I say Marigold. Anything wrong?" from father failed to penetrate the great heaviness of my soul.

At dead of night, I had got up and unlocked the door and stepped over the cold beans and sausages and gone to the bathroom and stood for ages looking in the glass, looking at my toothbrush wondering whether to brush my teeth, watching the toothpaste emerge from the tube and hang there. James Joyce. Then I put the brush and toothpaste down and went back along the silent landing, past father's door and the door to the Boys' Side, back to my own room, relocking the door and lying heavy and still again.

Next day I didn't get up. Paula's voice and Mrs Thing's floated into my consciousness now and then, sometimes raucous, sometimes cajoling, sometimes shrill. Aeons went by.

The cracks of light between the curtains had brightened and sharpened and spilled bright streaks over the carpet, then faded again to twilight, or summer midnight or grave-light or Styx light. The deep hollow in my pillow grew damp.

"Come on. A visitor, duck." Paula's voice came through rather different this time. It was sharp, not full of its usual Dorset vibrations. The criticism and the crossness had gone and instead there was – good gracious! There was fear. Paula frightened.

Oh no, no, no!

I heaved out of bed and blundered across the room to the key in the lock and began to turn it. Then I leaned my head against the door and stopped, like a machine run down. Through the door I heard whispers and quick conversation.

"No. Never. Never like this. Whatever happened over the road?"

"Nothing." (Grace Gathering's voice.) "Nothing. She was looking weird. She simply ran away."

"Ran away! Whatever from, dear sakes?"

"I don't know. We were coming forward over the grass – Ma and father and I and one or two. Some people of my parents, and Jack Rose – he'd been playing one-handed – and she suddenly became oh, absolutely – well, mad."

"Mad?" said Paula and I closed my eyes and started shaking.

"Mad? Marigold's not mad. That's one thing certain. Now look you 'ere young woman, I explained that to half a clutch of psychiatrists in Newcastle years back. Marigold's not mad. She's too sane, that's what's wrong with our Marigold. She sees clear and pure and sometimes it's a bit more than she nor anybody can bear."

"Oh but – "

"You watch your step calling Marigold mad."

"Oh I didn't – "

"You come precious near it. Precious near. Marigold's not just anyone, you know. Ho no. Just anyone can be mad. Almost everyone is a bit mad, seems to me. Not our Marigold. Just you mind – "

(Oh Paula I love you so.)

"Mad indeed, I never did!"

"But I never — " Poor old Grace. The flood gates were open.

"I've known Marigold since the minute her mother went and died on her and let me tell you she's the best and most uncommon creature."

(Why couldn't she have told that to me? Good gracious!) "All that eye-trouble, all that disapoplexia and whats thiz. Having to be read to. I've brought her up. I know her. She's the finest, straightest, brilliantest, no fancy nonsense neither."

I could just imagine what Paula must be looking like.

"Sorry. All right. Goodness me. I'm only saying what it looks like. Everybody says — Oh no! All right. Stop for heaven's sake. What I was going to say was that whatever you've done for her character you haven't exactly done much for her looks, have you?"

There was a sort of yell and so I opened the door and Grace who had been leaning against the other side of it fell backwards on to my floor and lay there. Paula and I looked down at her and even on the floor she looked graceful. Well named. She smiled up.

"Hi," I said.

"Well hullo," said she.

We established without the least self consciousness our first familiarity. I helped her up. "For instance," she said, "where did she get those pyjamas?"

Paula made a wild noise and thundered off out of sight. A door slammed.

"You know," said Grace, "you ought not to wear viyella pyjamas in brown and pink stripes and buttoned on the right. With a woven draw string."

"I've had them ages." I looked down and saw my legs sticking out from the knee downwards. My legs have been changing lately and it occurred to me, looking down that there was a lot more of them than there used to be. A good deal of arm hung out of each sleeve, too. "They've got *flies*," said Grace.

"They're from the Boys' Side. I expect Paula was using them up."

"Does Paula do all your clothes? Choose them?"

"Well she doesn't choose them exactly. When I need more she just looks round for something. There's usually something that'll do. She's very keen on being tidy and clean but – "

"I don't know what you mean by 'do'. If those pyjamas 'do'."

"Well nobody sees what you wear in bed do they?"

Grace looked at her pink fingernails for a minute. Then she walked to the window and drew back the curtains and flung the window up wide. She walked back and put out the light which I'd switched on. Seeing the bundle of clothes and the high-heeled blue shoes in the grate she walked over and stirred them with her foot. "That's good," she said, "Look, go and get washed."

"I got washed."

"When?"

"In the night." Then I remembered that I had merely examined the facilities.

"Wash again," said Grace.

"With a *clean* towel," she called down the landing, "and a nail brush and do your teeth."

I still couldn't use the toothpaste because of James Joyce but I washed all over. I got a new piece of purple-brown coal-tar which is so beautiful, in yellow paper, and I filled the basin utterly with hot water. I soaped myself all over to the knees then rinsed it off. Then I lifted one foot at a time into the basin and coal-tarred them, getting well in between the toes. A kind of ritual cleansing. I cut my toe nails with some scissors lying about and rubbed myself all over with one of father's brown towels with a red stripe at each end until I was very pink and blotchy. I had a very good go at my neck.

I wrapped the pale brown towel around me and another one out of the cupboard, picked up the pyjamas and went back to the bedroom where Grace was reclining gazing unashamedly into the windows of the big dormitory.

"They need some blinds in there," she said, "it's not a pretty sight. Good Lord – look at you! You look like a digestive biscuit. Give me those." She took the pyjamas by the tips of her fingers and dropped them on the heap in the grate. Then she shovelled the whole lot on to a bit of paper which seemed to be the lining of one of my drawers and made a big parcel. "Get some others," she said, "and come on. It's a quarter past four."

"Where are we going?"

"Shopping. Look — that'll do. That jersey and skirt thing and there's some pants — glory! Elastic legs! Shangri La."

"No — Lyme Regis."

"Well come on then — I hope the shops don't shut on Tuesdays."

"What shops?"

"Clothes shops."

She sailed through the dying chrysanthemums with the bundle under her arm and me running behind. Faces appeared all along the Boys' Side and there were some whistles. We met father at the gates who said, "Hello dear? Better then? Is this Grace?"

"We have to fly," said Grace, flowing on.

"To fly. Dear me. I'm not sure that's very wise."

We reached the street behind the High Street which is called Arthur Street — not a very well-thought-of street, full of purple brick houses with bay windows picked out in Bird's Custard brick. In one of these several pictures were displayed and some pink frilly curtains and the back of a hair dryer. A cardboard banner cried out CYNTHIA.

"I didn't know there was a hairdresser here."

"I found it last week."

"You've hardly been here a week. Hey — listen. I've never been to a hairdresser."

"She wants it cut," said Grace, "and *shaped*. Do you know how to layer?"

"Aye I do," said Cynthia who was muscular and had a bristling chin, "So don't come it over me. You lot" (it was the Dartington voice) "think we don't know owt up 'ere."

Grace, as bland as chestnuts, said, "A good *lot* off don't you think? Quite short and with a *shape*."

Great crunching noises took place around the back of my neck and orange blotches began to drop all over the floor. "Look," I said, "Paula — "

"Forget Paula. It's looking wonderful."

"Wonderful!"

"Yes wonderful."

Crunch crunch crunch.

"Aye it is that," said Cynthia. "Shall I wash it."

"No time. We've clothes to buy."

"Come back tomorrow. I'll set it up lovely in big rollers and give it a nice bit of back combing. It's a grand colour."

"Look," said Grace, and there I was with a sort of rusty flower on my head all curly bits. My face had a different shape and looked less bemused and I had grown a neck. My skull had a clean, oval shape. "You can cut hair," said Grace to Cynthia and the two of them nodded to each other in mutual respect. A little later we were tearing down the promenade to Marks and Spencers and Grace dropping the parcel of my old clothes into a litter bin that stood by the door. I said, "What about Oxfam?" but "Pity Oxfam," said Grace, "what have the destitute done to deserve those pyjamas?"

She sped about the counters picking up garments, dropping them in a heap beside the central cash desk. Now and then she looked at me and went off and burrowed for something else.

"We're on closin'," said the saleswoman.

"Won't be long," said Grace. There was a good deal of rattling of doors and bolts and counters began to be covered with dust sheets for the night.

"What size shoes d'you take?"

"Oh – fives."

"Look Miss, we're really shutting."

"These would do. Yes – I really think these would do."

"What – for me? Look Grace, where's the money – ? And wouldn't I break my neck?"

They were very high-heeled shoes but not like the old blue stilettos. They were criss-cross chestnut plastic with rounded toes and a strap over the top. They were a bit the colour of my hair. They had a lovely slinky way of going in near the instep. I got hold of one and it smelled wonderful.

"Miss – I'm sorry. If you don't finish I'll have to call in the authorities. My last bus to Dormanstown leaves in five minutes."

"All right," said Grace, "How much?"

There were five or six great big Marks and Spencers bags on the desk. "Will you take a cheque?"

"Eh? How old are you? Have you got a credit card?"

Grace produced one, then another.

"Yes – oh all right," she said. "Miss the Archers at this rate. Er –

79

Madam. It's twenty-six pounds." We were out in the street with all the bags and I had to clutch at the litter bin.

"*I* haven't got twenty-six pounds," I said.

"I have," said Grace. "I got it for you."

"Wherever from?"

"Hastings-Benson," she said, "Sweet old thing. He'll get it back from your Papa. I told him to put it around that you were a disgrace."

"A disgrace," I said when I was alone at home again, "A disgrace." Grace had swept away towards her own home and I had carried the great big crackling packages in. Before opening them I had had to eat. I had not eaten for twenty-four hours. I was faint, I was tottering. I stood in the kitchen and went all the way through a loaf of bread and a chunk of cheese and a bottle of milk and a bag of apples. Then upstairs again, tenderly, gently I drew out of the first bag the first garment.

Pair of jeans.

Next: skinny tee shirt.

Next: three-quarter length sage-green skirt. velvet. tight round hips.

Next: orange jersey colour of new hair.

Next – shoes. I put my face in them.

I put on the jeans and the jersey. Then I took them off and put on the velvet skirt and the shirt. Then I played around with a number of variations, as in chess. Then I put on the shoes and rose miles in the air. I looked in the glass, walking as far back from the mirror as I could and a tall thin girl with rather good legs and noticeable hair looked back at me. Her face was exalted. It was the face that was most surprising. I looked down and saw my glasses lying by the bed – great thick lumps. They had been lying by the bed since last night. I had been out shopping and had not even noticed. I had not needed them at all.

Chapter 10

So BEGAN MY half term of happy friendship with Grace Gathering.

"Whom do you think of marrying?" she asked out of the blue at the week end, decorating a long green talon.

We were over in the Head's House in her bedroom in the attics. Posters covered the walls. There was a hi-fi and coloured rugs, a bed draped with shawls and things and a row of old dolls. The dressing-table had an army of bottles of make-up and jars of cream. A mobile was stuck to the ceiling with bluetack. In my un-precedented jeans and shirt I sat at the dressing-table undoing bottles and smelling them and I grinned.

"What's the matter? Haven't you thought?"

"I haven't. But I was laughing at 'whom'."

"Whom?"

"'Whom do you think of marrying.' I was wondering how many people with green nails say 'whom'."

She looked blankly at me.

"All right," I said, "I just find it interesting. I've lived more in civilised society than you have."

"I wouldn't call Green's House society. It's hardly in the world. It's the most unworldly place — . I don't know how you stick it. I'm the normal one."

"I suppose so."

I looked round her room again. From television plays and a few people's conversation I could tell that it was normal, but to me

81

it was as familiar as a Tibetan monastery. In fact I would perhaps have felt a Tibetan monastery more ordinary, for my room and my father's room across the road were as bare as cells, with iron beds, grey blankets, one table each and a common denominational long shelf of books. The grate into which I had flung my clothes had never needed a fire. Well, it may have needed a fire but it had never been given one. I had never had dolls and if anyone had bought me a mobile I would not have known what to do with it.

There was however my upright piano and a picture of Winston Churchill in a sort of Chinese boiler suit. I don't know how that had got there, I had certainly had nothing to do with it. Looking round Grace's room with its huge poster of some young man gazing into a pool with indeterminate flowers growing all over the place and a slinky female eyeing him from across the bank I thought perhaps that I might take Winston Churchill down.

"D'you like it?"

"What?"

"Narcissus."

"Who?"

"The picture. Hasn't he got a marvellous spine?"

I looked quickly at the row of knobs and away. I still couldn't look at naked boys. I wondered for about the millionth time why Grace had been expelled from both Cheltenham and Dartington Hall.

"Go on. Look. He's heavenly."

"Not exactly heavenly," I said taking a quick glimpse through one eye.

"Put your glasses on. You can't see that close up without them. When are you going to get some decent ones?"

"I might. It's a bit of a waste – "

"Look – *make* your father buy you some. Edmund says he could. You don't have to wear all that National Health wiring. Get some gold ones. They're marvellous. People are buying them and putting plain glass in. They're dead fashionable."

"Dead fashionable," I said.

"What?"

"It's just – funny. With 'whom'."

"Look Bilge," she said, "Do shut up about words. Think of

what you look like. You may have poor eyes but other people haven't. It's anti-social. You look a million times better especially since you washed your hair, too, but you've got to keep *at* it. Looking good."

"Oh, it isn't worth it."

"Of course it is. Look — who do you think of marrying?"

"'Who' this time. Farewell Dartington Hall."

"They say worse things than who at Dartington Hall."

I left the dressing-table and lay on the floor and rolled about on it banging my head now and then into the sheepskin rug. I have noticed in literature that the physical movements of the young are seldom accurately described. Then I got up and pressed my face into the attic window. Boys walked below in twos and threes in their black blazers. It was windy. Leaves flew and spun. The pages of the exercise books under their arms whitened and flapped. The smaller boys ran and knocked each other about. Sometimes a master in a black balloon of a gown crossed the green grass towards the cloisters. A bell rang somewhere and the boys – some of them – began to run. Saturday morning school had a more light-hearted look about it than on weekdays and I watched it with, well – love I think – as my mind went about.

"You know," I said, "I don't much care for you saying 'Edmund'."

She painted another long nail and said, "You simply have not a clue about men, have you? You have no *feeling* for men."

"I wouldn't say that."

Jack Rose's figure appeared below, unmistakable in a First XV blazer and the Captain's segmented cap of black and white diamonds. He loped on his powerful legs and the minions scattered at his approach like Don John of Austria's. I got hold of Grace's window catch and clung on to it for support until my heart had stopped thundering.

"I wouldn't say that." This is the best conversation, I thought, the best and most promising and the most real that I have ever had in my life – and bother Paula and chess and character-building and silence. I have arrived. I am normal. I am like the others.

I wonder then, why am I saying nothing about where I am going at Half Term?

But I was not ready to go looking for an answer to this. I was not ready even to think about it myself. I had heard nothing more about it since Jack Rose had asked me the first week of term and though I had asked my father if he had had a letter from Mrs Rose and if so, please could he open it, I had the most extraordinary impediment in my speech about discussing things further. Father and I had hardly been apart from each other for a weekend in my whole life. To go to Jack Rose's without father, without anyone, seemed so unlikely and fanciful that I rather wondered if I had imagined the invitation altogether. The afternoon of its being handed out by Jack had been a very weird one – Terrapin sitting concussed in the changing rooms, not speaking. I had become a little concussed myself perhaps, just looking at him. I remembered telling Terrapin. Perhaps I had invented the whole thing just to annoy him? After all it was the afternoon of my nervous breakdown on the Headmaster's lawn.

But though I put the Half Term visit out of my mind I found that my interest in my new image had grown to immense proportions. Not a shop window down the High Street or the Prom. was free of my gaze and I looked endlessly at my hands. I twirled my feet. I wore the new shoes every day – even at school. I began to give a sort of toss to my head, quite spontaneously, at no fixed moment, accompanied by a half-closing of the eyes.

"Something wrong, Marigold?"

"No, Miss Bex."

"Are you in a draught?"

"No, Miss Bex."

"You look as if you have a stiff neck." In the corridor she put out a hand on my arm as I went by, "I shall be looking in on your father tonight."

"I like your shoes," said Aileen Sykes in a corridor stopping the coach momentarily en route to Versailles. "Where d'you get them?"

"Marks."

"They're great."

"I say — look at Bilge's hair," said Penelope Dabbs. "All fancy."

I wished we didn't have to wear uniform at school. I wished they could see the long orange cardigan. I wore it and an assortment of the rest of them — sometimes five garments at a time — about the House at home. In the evenings I walked slowly down through the gardens outside my bedroom window, very slow and tranquil and picked up Grace and together we strolled about the Playing Fields or along the Promenade, very slowly by the sea. Whistles and vulgar bellows emerged from the cafés and the dodgems as we went by.

"I say, you do get whistled at. Don't you notice it?" I asked Grace.

She smiled. "Perhaps they're whistling at you."

I would go to bed in a glow. I dazed into sleep. I did no work. Oxbridge was near. I paid no heed. I was the only one trying for Oxbridge but the rest of my form were all trying for somewhere and they were in torment. They were like the condemned with the eye on the axe, they were "terrified", they were "dying", they "hadn't a chance". They weren't going to "get in anywhere". They were learning up their notes each night, they were assailed by terrible dreams.

Not I, Bilgewater. I sank into my bed and the minute my eyes closed, there was Jack Rose and I striding behind him in the orange cardigan and a bronzy tweed skirt I hadn't yet actually got, two red setters at our heels over the purple moor, a castle in the background with butlers, and dancing till dawn. We walked like Titans or people out of *Country Life* into the sunset.

But it is funny. Neither Paula nor father nor Puffy nor Uncle Edmund Hastings-Benson seemed to notice a thing. I stood about in conspicuous places like the House steps at twilight. "Oh good," came Paula's voice from above, "Could you just run over to School Matron and get — "

Father drifting in from somewhere or other, seeing my new outline on the steps stopped and said, "Hullo. Are you wanting to speak to me? Oh Marigold, it's you! Didn't recognise you for a moment." I stood about the study on Thursdays looking the picture of experience and sophistication. "Glass of wine?" said Uncle Edmund, "Oh — sorry Bilgie. Thought it was Paula for a minute. Must be getting old.''

"D'you like my shoes?" (He always looked downwards at females.)

"Shoes? Splendid, splendid." He was even more abstracted than usual. "How's the new friend? Seen Grace lately?"

That evening I flounced off in exasperation towards the Fives Court and lingered there as I had never dreamed of doing, until the boys began to go in to bed. Nobody noticed me. It was a dark, blustery November evening and the wind got hold of my new tufts of hair and knocked them into spikes. Terrapin came by and looked at me, hard.

"What is it?" I said, "Don't you know me?"

"I know you," he said.

He was quieter, Terrapin, now and I noticed that he had grown most surprisingly tall and bony lately. His hair which had once hung like yellow matting was shorter and he was more lively looking. He wasn't in school uniform. He had a long skinny sweater on and long thin skinny denim trousers. His cheek bones stuck out. He looked like an Arthurian boy.

Terrapin an Arthurian boy? I must be mad!

"You look different." But it was I, Bilgewater speaking to him.

"I've torn my school trousers."

"Haven't you any more?"

"No," he said, "just these. What is it?"

"What's what?"

"I thought you wanted to say something."

"Me? No. Oh no. I was just going in."

"So'm I," he said, "I've a prose to do." He went off, unsmiling. I waited and I could have wept – at the stupidity of it, the pathetic, feeble, self-indulgent –

"D'you like my *hair*," I yelled, running after him. I could have hit him.

"I can't see it," he called in the dark.

Then he turned and came back. "Bilge – " he said, "This Grace – "

"Yes?"

"She won't do you any good."

"What d'you mean?"

86

"I don't know quite," he said, frowning, "I don't know. She's just not your sort. She'll make a mess of you."

"What *do* you mean?" I said and tossed my hair. "She's stopped me being a mess it seems to me."

"I liked you before," he said.

"First I'd heard of it."

He winced and I was reminded of Uncle HB when he said that I was vulgar.

"I did," he said. "I liked you. You were yourself then."

Chapter 11

SINCE THE TIME of the Abbot Wilfrid unlikely institutions have obtained at the school of his foundation. There is good historical evidence according to father of his being an unlikely man himself, packing in a hundred things at once where one or two would have been enough for most saints and earned them quiet sabbaticals of prayer and peace on one of the rocks along the coast for many a year to come, or south in clement Canterbury.

Wilfrid seems to have been a crack-on man, a man for throwing on a cloak and picking up a staff and setting off for face-to-face discussion. Always on the move – Ripon, Guisborough, York, north, south, up and up the one hundred and ninety-nine steps to the howling cliff top at Whitby and the high black walls of its abbey where Hilda his female counterpart, the first unmistakable Yorkshirewoman, awaited him to discuss synods and organisation and what to do with the holy Caedmon the herdsman who saw angels and sang songs about them in the local dialect.

Wilfrid, father had no doubt at all, accounted for the intense traditional activity in the school around the end of the Christmas term and the idiotic necessity for holding the school play, the school dance, the seven-a-sides at the same time as the Oxbridge entrance examinations – Hilda down the coast perhaps having pneumonia or being distracted by Caedmon or the pirates when it was all first arranged. Had she beeen consulted – or perhaps transported into the person of Paula – she would never have allowed such nonsense at all. "How can you expect," she would have said, "public examinations to take place in a hall which is at night used for the production of a panto and the next evening – the first day of the Oxbridge Scholarships – for the Annual St Wilfrid's Grand Dance?" And only a man of the most appalling energy would then have arranged for the Rugby matches to take place the day after, knowing that three-quarters of the team all in hard training were likely also to be examinees.

For the first time, the November of my transformation, a decision was taken about this proliferation, and taken for a wonder at one of father's Thursdays. I happened to be present because I had been called down to speak to Miss Bex who had looked in again about something to do with my syllabus and Paula said if I went to say goodbye to her perhaps it would get her off.

She had now gone.

The subject of conversation was the ancient and immemorial one in that room of the ability of boys.

"Wilson? Fool."

"I wouldn't say that. I wouldn't say that."

"Three Cs and an E, he won't make Surrey."

"Good chance in the re-take."

"Not a hope. Day boy. Knocking about the streets."

"Glegg then?"

"Worse. Hull if he's lucky."

"Sykes?"

"Pretty sister," said Uncle Edmund HB. "Won't do anything though. Lives in Pearson Street."

"They used to say," trembled old Price, "that the people in Pearson Street have blacklocks in their cake tins."

"There are curious things in Oxford and Cambridge cake tins," said Puffy. "What about Rose, H-B?"

"Oh a dead cert. A dead cert. Solid chap. All-round fellow."

"Not so sure," father frowned.

"Great Scot, William, if Rose went to bits – "

"He might. It's happened. Remember Wellington-Wells."

Long silence while Wellington-Wells's extraordinary failure to reach Oxford in 1910 is contemplated once again.

"Oh Rose'll be all right," said Puffy.

"Terrapin?"

"Now there's an interesting one. Anything might happen. Odd chap."

"I'm growing interested in Terrapin," said Puffy, "There's a great deal there. He used to be so very plain. What do you think, William?"

"Eh?" said father, "Terrapin?"

"You know him best. More or less lived here all his vacations when he was a junior didn't he? Some trouble at home."

"Mmmm," said father. You can get nothing out of him in what he feels to be a private matter. "Marigold," he said, "Oughtn't you to be in bed — or doing some work of some sort?"

But I hung about the door pretending to look at the chess.

"He's grown up lately — that's what it looks like to me. More able to take things," said Uncle Edmund.

"He's had a lot to take," said father almost in an aside, corkscrew searching. "He is a very gifted — aha. Yes. Here we are."

"Well he's no rugger player or dancer and he's not in the play so he may do you credit," said Uncle Edmund. "Get some sleep. God knows how many scholarships we lose through this idiotic Christmas socialising. Can't see why we can't at least get rid of the dance. Or get the damn thing over early."

"We can't this year," said Puffy. "Hall's still being decorated."

"Well, hold it somewhere else."

"Where?"

"On the pier."

"On the *pier*! Good God man, the saints would turn in their graves."

"I don't see why. I don't suppose there was a dance at all when the school was an abbey. Can't see all those monks giving the boys a Christmas twirl."

"I remember the pier the night of the zeppelins — " Price began and was astonishingly interrupted by father saying, "You know — Why *not* hire the pier? It would be rather jolly. I like piers."

" — all little bundles of flame dropping into the sea — "

"If it was on the pier I think I'd go."

"You might GO!" I cried from the door.

"Yes. Yes." He had quite forgotten I shouldn't be there. "Yes.

90

Why not? I might enjoy a dance."

"Good heavens!"

"I always used to go you know when your mother was alive." (Uncle HB dropped his chin upon his chest.) "Yes. I'd rather like a dance."

The effect of this was twofold in that first I reeled away to my bedroom and sat before some work for an hour doing it like a rather cheap calculator that needs re-charging, and thinking all the time "Father! *Father*! Horrible. Indecent!", and second that I then went off to find Grace and tell her.

"Terrapin interesting! Terrapin brilliant. Terrapin having much to bear. Terrapin grown up" was what I meant to discuss. Yet for some reason when I reached Grace's room I didn't. I only mentioned the saga of the dance. I decided to lead the conversation round to Terrapin again on Sunday when father, Paula and I always have lunch together.

Father was in one of his more usual moods – that is to say he was looking as if he wanted to fly into the stratosphere and consider the meaning of meaning and Paula and I were peacefully at ease with him and some excellent Yorkshire pudding.

"D'you think that Terrapin's got different lately, Paula?"

"I do not."

"They say he's changed."

"He has not."

"They say he's matured."

"Whatever does that mean? Cheese matures."

"Well don't people?"

"There's several opinions."

"He's less ugly."

"Whatever's that got to do with it? Whatever's looks – ?" Her eyes flashed and her hair swayed.

"You don't know what it's like to be plain," I said.

"Now leave off that. BEWARE OF SELF PITY. Mind, I begin to understand it, lookin' at that show."

"What show?"

"That tatter-heap atop of the head."

"It's a feather cut." I shook it. In fact I was delighted. At least and at last she had noticed.

"Cost a pound so it's rumoured. Around the bazaar."

"Well father paid. He didn't mind. I've got it. Mother left me some. Grace found out from Uncle HB. My *mother*," I said, "knew what a young girl would need."

"Didn't do her much good," said Paula, "You don't need hair-cuts in heaven."

"Well I'm not – "

"Nor likely to be. Dear Lord! Looks!"

"He is very remarkable," said father finishing the apples and custard and flying down from somewhere round the back of Hayley's comet. "In my view. Possibly – is there any more?"

"No. I did ask you."

"Custard?"

"Too late."

"Who're we talking about?" I asked.

"Well Terrapin. Tom Terrapin. D'you know, Paula, Marigold, just between the three of us I think Tom Terrapin may be the cleverest, most original boy I've ever taught." He sat back and gave us his smile.

"Then he'll likely miss a scholarship," said Paula who knows more about boys and examinations than any University Board. Her sick-room and the San are stripped for action in examination weeks with all the beds turned down, hot water bottles at the ready, though in fact hardly any of them need them after a short burst of her wisdom and incisive reflections at the idiocy of judging anyone by some bits of paper scribbled down in a few hours when the balance of the mind is disturbed. Father says anyway that you can't judge anybody's real ability until after the second Degree.

"That is not the point," said father, "I wasn't talking of scholarships. I was talking of Terrapin. He might be. I think he might be – um, aha, something. Marigold," he said with the same air of apparent logic that honestly does make him a very trying man, "Why don't you ask him to the dance?"

Chapter 12

THE PIER PAVILION is a long, wooden yellow shack on the landward
end of the pier which trails a little way seawards and then drops
down towards the water in a mess of black and broken spikes. A
ship had hit the pier in the war – it is the most undramatic and yet
treacherous piece of coast so flat that from out to sea you can't see it
at all and unwary sailors think they may have made a mistake and
crunch up on to the shelf of rock that runs out just beneath the cold,
grey water that has made havoc since the Vikings. There is a chain
across the pier about a hundred yards beyond the back of the
pavilion and beyond this nobody goes.

Most of the pavilion is on dry land but at the back towards the
stage the boards beneath your feet grow cold and you can look
down between the cracks and see the sea whitening rhythmically
beneath you. When I was a small child I once went to a horrible
fancy-dress dance there and sat alone for hours on a tip-up red
velvet seat round the side of the ball room, glaring through my
glasses at all the fairies and clowns, decked out myself in whatever
it was that Paula had found for me at the last minute, speaking to
no one. All that I really knew of the pier was the hell of that
evening and the terrors of the final parade: that and the cracks with
the sea underneath, and the great tumult of the band.

But I had a distinct conviction nevertheless that the Pier
Pavilion was not much of a place – even then, and it must be much
more battered by now. I passed it when I walked home from school

and fish and chip papers scraped around its doors. Pop music, flashy lights and vomiting locals hung about its shadows of a Saturday night, unbeautiful among the tilted fishing boats drawn up outside upon the promenade and the swash and glimmer of the sea and the shore beyond. It was a real rough dive.

Yet Grace when she stopped me at school on the corridor between lessons seemed delighted.

"Have you heard?" she said, "It's fixed. The pier."

"What! The Old Boys' Dance?"

"My father OK'ed it yesterday. It's to be just before Half Term so's to get it over before all the Christmas flap."

"Have you *seen* it?" I said.

"The pier? Of course I've seen it."

I remembered the pink hairdresser's and how she'd found that when she had hardly been in the town a couple of days. I had a decided fancy, all of a sudden, that Grace knew the pier quite thoroughly.

"You don't mean you've been there?"

She smiled from the heights.

"Good heavens — Awful people — " I thought of Aileen Sykes and Beryl. They were the sort. Bare mid-riffs. Purple lips. Someone once told me that Beryl's mother worked there at the ticket office — eating biscuits and knitting. A wave of loyalty to ancient St Wilfrid's flooded over me.

"This'll be a private dance," I said, "I don't see the pier being the place for a *private* dance."

"Do you go to many private dances?" asked Aileen Sykes weaving up. "Northanger Abbey I suppose."

"I just — No — I'm just surprised," I said, "I don't see it being all that — partyish — at the pier."

Aileen went into hysterics and Grace turned her head aside for a minute. "Honestly," she said, "Bilgewater — honestly!"

"I don't see anyone going, that's all," I said. "It's smelly and cold there. The Old Boys are getting on — some of them."

"Never met any meself," said Beryl. "I'm only going since it's the pier. I go every Saturday."

"*You're* going!"

I couldn't help it. She is so huge and greasy. You can tell she

94

never washes her tights. "My *father's* going," I said.

It nearly gave them apoplexy.

"Thank goodness anyway," I said, "that I am not," and I stuck to this through the next couple of weeks with unshakeable firmness. "Oh go on, Bilgewater," they said – almost half the form. It was the big joke. Hair, shoes, orange cardigan, I was still the big joke. Everybody far and near had decided to go to the St Wilfrid's Dance since it was at the pier and not in the ancient cloisters.

"No."

"Why not?"

"I can't dance. I hate the pier."

"Go on. It's great."

"It's not."

"Why?"

"It's – sad," I said.

"Go on – cheer it up then." They were all on about it, morning, noon and night. Dinner time. On the bus. Whom they were going with. They had even stopped talking about the exams.

"And that shows *something*," said Paula. "It's a wise idea to have it now. Gets their minds cleared."

"I'll keep mine cluttered then," I said, "I'm not going."

"Well I am," said Paula, "I love a dance."

"At the pier!"

"Snob," she said. "Watch your motives. For all the world a Victorian aunt now. Like your mother. *She'd* never have gone to the pier."

I thought of the hat brim, the delicate chin, the string of amber beads in the photograph. Ladies in amber beads used to organise the fancy dress balls when I sat on the tip-up velvet seats. I all at once remembered. I remembered the way they used to sail about, these ladies holding glass ice-dishes, poising their tea spoons high. The picture was graceful and pleased me.

"I don't know, Marigold. I don't know," said Paula in a voice all earthy and tired. "I don't know what to make of you."

On the day, she ran into my room about five where I was doing some Applied at my table and said, "You are going to come, my lover, aren't you?"

"I told you. No thanks."

"Oh Marigold."

"It's no good. I'd loathe it."

"How do you – That Grace is going. And your hair's lovely just now."

"Very interesting," I said. "The sudden revelation to Paula of the loveliness of Bilgewater's hair."

"I always told you it would be – "

"Oh, shut up," I said, "It's back nearly where it was anyway. The fringe is grown out. I'm not going."

At eight the phone rang and after they'd all bellowed and yelled I answered it. "Are you ready yet?" asked Grace.

"I'm not going. I told you."

"Oh don't be silly." Her voice went up high and Dartington and I could see her grand and noble profile in my mind, the excellent, easy, well-bred sort of way she crossed her legs and leaned back holding the phone, "I'll call for you."

"I'm working."

"Jack Rose was asking if you – "

"I AM WORKING."

"We'll *both* call for you."

I put down the phone and sat down at the desk. I couldn't concentrate one bit. There was a knock at the door and in came father.

"Well now."

"Hullo."

"Aha."

Silence.

"Well now, Marigold, what about this dance?"

I turned and it was a fearful sight – a bow tie. Hair smoothed down. Dinner jacket brought over with the zeppelins. A sort of cheery grin.

"Save us and help us – "

"Now now my dear."

"We humbly beseech Thee Good Lord."

"Marigold – it seems a pity. Just as you're beginning to have a few friends and looking so nice."

"I've a lot to do."

"You don't need to," he said. "There is time yet. You have covered the ground. You can over-prepare for Oxbridge you know. Cambridge especially doesn't just rely on the papers. It's the interview that counts."

"If the papers aren't right you don't get an interview. If you're a girl anyway."

"Ah – I shouldn't worry. You know – " he screwed up his face and bent over my work. "Greek to me," he said after a bit and then laughed. "I wonder why you *didn't* choose Classics. I could have helped then. But you will be all right. That nice Miss Box – "

"Bex."

"Bex. It's an unusual name. Charming woman though."

"Bex!!"

"Jack Rose asked me this evening if you were coming," he tried once more, at the door, "It'll be very quiet all alone here."

"Go."

He went.

"Why couldn't he have asked me himself then?" I said out loud five minutes later. Asking Grace about me. Asking Father. When Paula's trumpet calls had ceased and the front door of the House slammed to, I got up and went and looked out of the window. All the dormitory windows of the Boys' Side were dark and silent. The winter garden, rose bushes like barbed wire, was empty under the moon.

"Not as though he found handing out invitations exactly difficult. He's pretty good at forgetting them afterwards." I dropped the curtain and went and looked at the grate for a while.

"'My mother used to know your mother'. Oh splendid. Likely story."

I went on with the Applied for a while and ate an apple and some bread I had around and pulled open a tin of Coca Cola and sloshed it about, listening to it inside. I did a bit more work. Then I walked around and went to the piano and played a few bars of Bach and stopped. It was intensely, eerily quiet, the great House so used to the noise of boys and Paula, was still as something undiscovered in the Valley of the Kings.

Good night for a burglar, I thought, and then I heard a noise outside the door on the landing. It was the noise of slow and rather thoughtful breathing.

We haven't a dog. It certainly wasn't one of the cats. The cook and housekeeper were away and all the junior boys, too young for the Old Boys' Dance, had been sent over to School House where the young boarders of the whole school were being hoarded together playing billiards and horsing about with old School House matron who was about a hundred and twelve and her dancing days well done.

"Hullo?" I called.

There was no reply but the breathing went on and there was a creak outside as of someone easing their feet. I went over to the door and locked it and stood by it, gazing at the panels as if they would turn to glass in a minute and I would see through.

I said, "Hullo?" again and thought I heard someone say "Bilge," quietly.

Then I went all hot up the back of my neck and tears came into my eyes and my hands began to shake. I leaned my forehead on the door panel and unlocked it again. I thought, He hasn't forgotten. He hasn't. It's him. He's come to fetch me. "Jack?" I said.

But it was Terrapin standing outside my room, very solemn in the shadows.

"Why're you here?"
"Why're you?"
"I'm working."
"Oh."

We stood in the great silent building looking into each other's eyes. His round blue ones were blank and rather frightening. How he had changed from long ago.

"D'you want to come in?"
"I just came to see you."
"The Boys' Side's all dark."
"I was – I wasn't there. I saw your light."

"My father –" I said, and surprised myself as when I had told him about Rose's queer invitation to stay, "My father, of all people has gone to the dance. At the *pier*!"

"The pier," he said again. He said it slowly. "A dance on the

98

pier." I knew he had the same feeling about it as I had.

"D'you not want to go? With him there?"

"No," I said. "Yes."

"Come with me."

"D'you want to go?"

"No."

"Then — ?"

"You should. You should."

"Why me?"

"Because it is damaging for you to be so much alone."

"And you?"

"I — " he said. He looked round my room over my shoulder. "This is a dull place," he said. "And I'm not alone really. Or at any rate it doesn't matter." He pushed me aside and walked all round my room, touched the piano keys, touched a box, the picture of my father, looked without enthusiasm at Winston Churchill. At the window he lifted the curtain and looked across at the Boys' Side. "I see it," he said, "I suppose as you do." He looked over at the row of tall Georgian windows for a long time, then down at the stark garden. "Oh Bilge, Bilge," he said.

I watched him — every spare bone of him and almost wept because I was longing so much for someone else — someone confident and rounded and cheery. When Terrapin turned, his cheek bones seemed to stick out like set-squares.

"Let's go to the pier."

"I couldn't. I couldn't."

"I don't mean to the dance, fool. Let's go to the pier. Get a coat."

I was in the orange cardigan, skirt and the shoes.

"*You* haven't a coat."

"I never feel cold. Get a coat."

There was one of Paula's or someone's just inside the front door and I slung it on and we set off. He loped and swooped ahead through the garden and down the quiet High Street, past the Town Clock and along the promenade. The pier was at the far end of it, a mile away. The cliffs of the treacherous coast lifted their heads beyond but unseen here behind the blue glare of the Bingo parlours and fruit machines and bumpum shops. After some distance Terrapin striding ahead of me stopped and pounced across the road, through the fishing boats, down a stone slope and on to the sands and became at once invisible in the darkness. I followed but he had quite disappeared.

"Terrapin," I called, "Terrapin."

The sands — great white sands beneath the moon and breathtaking blue sky with bluer clouds sliding fast over the stars — the sands were firm and brilliant under my feet. They were wide and empty and I trudged over them until after ages — they are famous sands, enormously wide and hard — I reached the edge of the whitening sea.

I watched it. Now and then again it approached and became transformed into curled white foam, ceased at my feet and withdrew. Far, far away towards Norway was the long dark blue line of the horizon.

"Terrapin."

At an angle far across the sands his or someone's figure slid away and in the bright moonlight I scurried after it. We drew nearer to the promenade again and after a time the jagged and unlikely slope of the pier rose up before us — or rather before me because Terrapin's figure had gone again somewhere under the black geometry of spars. I went in after him and stood among the big crossed metal rafters — the rush of the sea on my left and the land-sounds on my right. I looked up and saw that I was under the pier floor — long gold lines of light stretched like pencil strokes above my head, and I could hear the beat of the band. There was an occasional shriek and laugh but otherwise the silence under the pier was the silence of the dungeon. And Terrapin was gone.

I walked under the pier and then up the steps to the sea-wall and round to the entrance. There were two turnstiles, the fish and chip papers aforementioned and in abundance, and a little ticket office in the middle with a light on, but not a bright one, and a firmly shut door. I looked in at the ticket office and wondered whatever to do next. Terrapin must be somewhere.

The office was minute — so small that it looked like an upright coffin or a box a doll might arrive in for a birthday, if one were given such things. One looked for strings to hold the doll upright. It was a mummy-case but there was no mummy inside it. Instead there was a cup of tea on the little shelf where one slid one's ticket or money across – old-looking tea with a thickish surface. There was a young woman in the box but she was turned away and bent over and she was turned away because she was heaving at a huge fat woman who had fallen on the floor.

Not even on the floor. She had no opportunity to fall even satisfyingly upon the floor. She had fallen half way to it by stooping, perhaps by trying to reach her sandwiches from a bag, perhaps by trying to ease off her shoes. Like a great, stuffed draught-excluder or bolster she was bent over with her face turned up to me with a stupid and yet cunning look, and the younger woman had her arms round the poor thing's waist and was giving vigorous and rather desperate heaves. "Mother's stuck," she said, "Eeeh dear!"

"Er – can I do anything?"

"Put it on the shelf."

"I beg your – "

"Put the ticket money on the shelf. I'll get her up directly."

"Can't I come round and – if I could get the door open – "

The older woman gave a huge wheeze at this point and still turned her great face up towards me. The sound was like air escaping from a rubber ring. One waited for her to flatten.

"Git on," said the woman, "I'll manage. She's had a fall. Fifty p. if you're not a ticket-holder."

"Pffffffffffff," said the bolster woman and suddenly collapsed out of sight. "Eeeh dear," said the other, "Father said don't tek 'er. She'll not be comfortable he said. She said it was just for company, but eeh dear she's gettin' dreadful. It's a funny thing but wherever she goes, things happen!"

I flung down some money by the cup of tea and rushed through the swing doors and round the side of the kiosk into the great battery of the band. There were people all around me all dressed up with glasses in their hands, laughing and leaning against each other. There was no one I knew – no Terrapin.

"Terrapin!" I shrieked and looked round for some way of getting at the back door of the ticket office. If I could find it, if I could only fling it open and let the fat woman roll out! I was terrified, shocked by the great person, doubled up, wheezing, watching me with such a curious, animal eye, like the eye of fate.

"Bilgie!"

"Oh please, please – " It was of course, and thank God, Jack Rose.

"Rose, Rose – " I said. "Oh something horrible – "

"Why, Bilgie!"

"Oh horrible – in the kiosk. There's a woman ill. Suffocating. Oh, help her."

"Kiosk, Bilgie?"

"The ticket office. Oh quick. Quick." I began to pull at doors here and there – a cloakroom, a W.C., a rather dreary kitchen where people were arranging lettuce on plates. "Oh Rose there's something horrible."

With me running behind he began to clear a path through the couples in the foyer and out again on to the promenade. "Where?" he asked.

"The ticket office. The kiosk."

We looked in. The younger woman was sitting with her knitting. The great bolster with the sideways face was gone.

"Your mother!" I cried. "Is she all right?"

"Fifty p.," said the knitter, "if you've not got tickets."

"But where's your *mother*? She was stuck on the floor."

The woman gawped.

"You said she was having an attack – "

"Eh?"

"Now come along back, Bilgie," said Jack Rose, "come along now."

"But she was. She was terrible."

"Imagination Bilgie. Come on."

"She couldn't breathe. She couldn't move."

"Come on in and join Grace and everyone. Your father's here. Marvellous evening." I noticed how small his eyes were again and how confident his face. There was a beer glass in his hand at a bit of a tilt.

"She was *suffocating*."

"Come on Bilge." He staggered a bit at the door and his hand – a great big hand – fell heavily across the back of my hips. It was pretty hot.

"You don't understand," I wept (and nor did I) and I fled through the wooden paintless foyer of the pier and out on to the dance floor where the world had run mad. I saw Paula with her hair bobbing like Africa and Mrs Gathering in a great deal of dark silk, Uncle HB at arm's length and in ecstasy with Grace, faces, faces – Miss Bex – Miss *Bex* – revolving in a long red pinafore – and Aileen Sykes pressed cheek to cheek against – oh no! oh no! Cheek to skin against Terrapin.

There was a door half way down the ballroom labelled FIRE EXIT with two great bars across it saying push. I stretched out my hands like a sleep-walker and made for it, running, reached it, pushed and exploded into the night, on to the deck of the pier out of the bedlam and into peace. I leaned back as the doors clattered shut behind me, clutched the anonymous coat round myself and wept.

But why? I thought after a bit, why am I so unhappy? An old fat nasty woman stuck in a box and Terrapin dancing with Aileen Sykes. What's it got to do with me? It doesn't matter. I drifted along the pier, down to the warning chain. After a bit I heard footsteps behind me on the narrow white boards so I dipped under the chain and went on down the pier on to the dangerous part and to where the wood ended and the broken spars began.

The footsteps came on and so I went on, too, until the pier ended in the two spiked horns of metal that ended in muddle and devastation where the ship had snapped them to pieces. The bars underfoot here were wide apart and the sea below was silken, swelling and very near.

To the side was a rickety spiral of metal, a sort of staircase or companionway twisting down towards the water – a place perhaps for boarding a boat long ago, a rescue point – somewhere they had set out to look for the poor men in the zeppelins – a place for descent to big boats that need deep water and for the disentanglement of lines. When I reached the head of this staircase that ended in the water I stopped.

Terrapin came up behind me in the dark and said, "Go down."

"I can't."

"Go on down."

He gave me a bit of a push and I found myself going down.

103

Each little narrow iron step had a pattern of holes in it with the gleam of the sea coming through them. He followed and when we were well down, far below the pier, we came to a little iron platform and stopped. He came up behind me on the platform and held me steady, like a gangster, his arms down over mine and we stood together with the deep water underneath us and the top of my head beneath his chin. He was all bones. "Watch," he said.

In a minute, beyond the end of the broken pier, the sea rose up in a wall and began to move towards us in a great black slippery curve with lines of spittle down its back, very fast. It approached, it reached us, it plunged under us, it passed by. The iron staircase swung and groaned. Cold water covered our feet and spray soaked into us. The wave passed on and we heard it break far behind us under the pier where the music played. I shouted out, "Where did you go? I saw something horrible. I saw you dancing with — "

He said, "Hush. Watch again."

Again the sea raised itself up and charged. Again it went for us, snarled, grabbed, passed by. Again it broke behind us.

"Terrapin — why — ?"

"It's wonderful," he said, "I love it."

"Terrapin. I'm frightened."

"Frightened. Frightened. Always frightened. Go on then."

He let me go and I fled up the stairs and crawled up on to the swinging metal floor of the pier above. He followed and stood beside me. "Bilge," he said, "Marigold.

"Marigold, you really must move on. Grow up."

I was crying I think. I don't know what I was doing. I was waiting for him to hold out his hand.

He held out his hand, "Oh Marigold, Marigold."

"Hullo," called a voice, "Who's there?" Jack Rose approached. "Keep quite still," he boomed. "All right. Don't move. Nothing to be afraid of."

"My God," said Terrapin and made off. Rose came up and heaved me to my feet. "Bilge? All right now. Don't panic. Hold on to me." His large form towered and he sounded very admirable and assured. I smelled the beer again as he heaved me up on to my feet, fastening my hands on to the rail of the pier. "Look over there, old thing — over towards the land. Don't panic. Bear up.

However d'you get out here? Too much booze? It's a great party — great night."

"It's not *that*," I said.

"And look at this step-ladder, spiral staircase what have you? God, how dangerous! Look it's held on by two screws. Hundred years old. Have some fool going down there next. Look – "

There were two big raised round screws holding the staircase to the side of the damaged pier. The holes they were in were rusted, the threads beneath – huge and rusty, too – were nearly worn away. "By God," said Rose, "This could be *lifted* off. Look." He gave a crazy sort of shake and shove and the whole staircase fell sideways held by one screw only. "Look at this then," said Rose with another shake.

"No don't," I cried, "No don't. It's nice. Don't."

But he gave a great tug at the bolt on the second screw and there was a creaking, squealing noise like faulty brakes on a very big lorry. "A-hey!" he called, triumphant and happy, authorised to command and destroy. A fine and happy fellow whatever befell.

"Watch this!" and the whole staircase suddenly loosened itself and fell sideways, heavily into the sea, quite slowly. Its splash was swallowed in the next great wall of oncoming wave. Where the stairs had been was only a space in the railings opening on nothing. "What do you know!" he cried and bending down he got hold of me in his arms, jubilant. He hugged me, enraptured with himself and all his cleverness. His face was very smooth and large as he kissed me and I thought, This is Jack Rose and this is I, Bilgewater, but all I wanted to do was look back at the space where the lovely metal steps had led down into the water.

Chapter 13

THE GREAT DISCUSSION on how to get me there was over in the end only when Paula stood waving me off at the Playing Fields bus-stop. The whole of the previous Thursday evening soirée had been given over to resolution of the difficulties of the undertaking which had at first seemed insurmountable. Half Term began on Saturday morning, but Jack Rose who had at first said that I was to travel with him, was playing a badly-arranged away match that afternoon and would be approaching his home for the holiday from another direction. It had not been suggested that I go with the team to watch the match, which was at least something to be thankful for. "Doesn't Boakes or someone live in that direction? There must be someone she could travel with?" But Boakes and everyone not in the Rugger team wanted to be off early on the Saturday morning.

Jack's home was over twenty miles away beyond Teesside, north of Middlesbrough and involved changes on the bus at unknown and seedy-sounding halts. For years and years boarders of St Wilfrid's had been arriving at no more than thirteen or fourteen and getting themselves off home again at end of term and half term with phlegm and confidence. Yet here was I at nearly eighteen causing everybody the keenest anxiety.

On Thursday morning Puffy Coleman had been over to Scar-borough Public Library and the bus station for timetables. Uncle Edmund had spoken of getting his car on to the road again – he had been planning to do this at Half Term, he said. He could make a trial run. Father said that since Rose was not available I had perhaps better not go at all. He said that in his opinion it was usually a mistake to go away and that I had always been perfectly content at home at Half Term before. I agreed with him at once, and with wonderful relief and gratitude. It now seemed incredible that I had turned to water when Rose had first invited me, that I had boasted to Terrapin about it and been so overcome with joy by it all that I had been unable to mention it to Grace. I settled down to finding the Roses' telephone number in the House files and planning to get Paula to ring up and say I had got bubonic plague. It would be rude of course, especially as, between the lot of us, we had only just got round to answering Mrs Rose's invitation and then only on the telephone when she had rung up to see what was happening.

I had answered the phone to a vibrant and not altogether sympathetic voice which said it wanted to speak to me and, remembering my moronic efforts at managing Mrs Gathering, I had replied with a sort of feeble bleat which implied that I would put the call through to father. "For what we are about to receive," he said to Mrs Rose, "let us be truly thankful," for he had been about to take Boys' Supper and the extension had rung on the sideboard behind him. He had picked it up thoughtlessly imagining it to be the Lord. The vibrant noises emerged from the earpiece and all the boys stood poised wondering whether they should get down to the mince and beans.

"Sit. Sit," said father.

Squawks of celestial surprise came out of the phone.

"How lovely," said father. "Yes, I'm sure she'd love to come. Invitation? No, I don't think so. Three weeks ago? Oh dear." With the hand not holding the telephone he began to beat at the outside of all his pockets, and then, as the squawks gathered pace slowly to empty the contents of the more accessible ones on to the table cloth.

"The post is so uncertain," he said as pieces of chalk, biros, paper clips, confiscated Mars-bars and several pairs of spectacles mounted beside the cooling mince. "She has been doing the first of her Cambridge entrance papers. It *may* have been delivered of course. Things get put on my desk and I am not told of them. Then they put piles of exercise books down – (he was scrammelling in the bottom of a remote pocket somewhere under an armpit and now brought out a very exhausted-looking envelope) "I really am so very sorry – (opening the envelope and looking stricken) My dear Mrs Rose I shall see to it at once and of course she may come. How very kind of you to ask her!"

But now, Friday night, he and I had both lost our nerve. The weather outside the study window was particularly vile – sweeps of grass had become mud, gaunt rugger posts stood up to a pitiless gale with ferocious, flying clouds and black firewood trees straining inland against it. Father's fire shone bright, three cats sat at angles to one another on the hearth-rug and the chessmen looked very inviting, an oasis of promise in the warm muddle of the room.

But, "Now she's to go!" said Paula. "If I take her myzelf she's to go. Whatever d'you think could befall her, dear Lord!" After Thursday's arbitration she had whirled in, seized Puffy's timetable, extracted the Saturday bus service, telephoned the Roses and pressed a very dreadful dress of olive green wool with ginger zig-zags and laid it on the end of my bed.

"Wherever did that come from?"

"It's one I've had by me."

"Well I'm not wearing that. I'm going in my jeans."

"Jeans! You can't go in jeans. It's a doctor's house. They'll change their clothes for supper."

"Perhaps they'll change into jeans. I don't see why they should change though at all. Doctors don't get all that filthy. Is it a slum or something? I thought it was a country house."

"I've no notion what it is except that it's beyond Marston Bungalow. There's some very good houses out beyond Marston Bungalow. All doctors have to change for dinner on account of the germs."

"Paula," I said, "Where on earth do you get your ideas from?"

"I've lived a long time. I'm a middle-aged woman. In Dorzet – "

"Dorset must be a fairly funny place – all the doctors taking their clothes off – "

"That'll do. Anyway, if you wear this nice patterned wool you won't need to change at all. You can wear it the whole weekend.

It's a dress," she said, "that will take you anywhere."

She harangued on and I felt in the end whatever anyway does it matter? I felt it simultaneously with the memory of Jack Rose's large, smooth face, the eyes that would never see what anyone was wearing anyway. Some breath of uneasiness stirred. I had had the same feeling when he had laughed at the falling iron stairs; and there was something else. I turned my mind away.

"OK," I said. "Forget it. I'll wear it I suppose," and on Saturday morning I put it on, slowly, masochistically and regarding myself in the glass. I hadn't bothered to go to the pink hairdresser again and the hair-cut was now certainly growing out. I hadn't bothered to go and see Grace again since the dance either, and she hadn't bothered to come and see me. I hadn't bothered to buy the Revlon Touch and Glow I had passed in the chemist on my way to a long meditation on the sands. I hadn't de-haired my legs like Aileen and Beryl did so disgustingly but with good effect in the cloakrooms when they were off gym. I had been working pretty steadily at the Oxbridge and reading in the intervals for extra agony the book Terrapin had left in my room the night of the dance (called *Prometheus Unbound* by Aeschylus trs.).

I was in a funny mood altogether. I put on my shoes – I could not quite bring myself to leave the shoes – pushed some washing things and pyjamas in a small suitcase Paula lent me and said, "All right then. I'm dressed."

"I will have to do," I said waving Paula goodbye. She stood looking very fine and fearless at the bus-stop, plumed like a war horse. She has narrow shoulders and hips and long long legs as well as a fantastic neck. She could have been a real goddess, a figure of justice, empress or Boadicea. Her wave was very assured and grand, telling me that there was nothing to fear. Why then, I wondered did I feel so awful? Why were my eyes hot and tears running down the back of my nose all the time, and why was I turning and blowing more steam on to the window and not caring who sat next to me or what happened to the landscape nor about anything in the world?

Soon however I was aware that something very large and heavy was sitting beside me, or rather spilling and swelling all over me, creaking and heaving about on the rattling double seat. I tried to think of important matters. I tried for instance to think what it would have been like if it had been my mother waving me off on the bus. I imagined her, little and sweet in a sort of cape with a hood, bits of silvery, silky blonde hair blowing out under it, both small hands pressed up against her mouth, tears in her eyes.

"Oh Marigold, it'll seem such *ages* till you're back. You're sure you'll be all right?"

"Of course I will. Really Ma!"

"I know it's silly but you do *hear* such things. You're so pretty. Some awful man might try and pick you up. Look you do know about – well, I just don't know what to say about these new ideas about – well sex and so forth, but – "

"For goodness sake mother! I'm not a baby. It's not even Jack Rose who's asked me – it's his *mother*."

"Oh Marigold I'm *dying* to know all about it. Do write. I know it's only three days."

Or – No. It wouldn't be like that. Mother would be in an Aston Martin. She'd have that marvellous long, turned-under, young-looking white hair, and lipstick and she'd be wearing a heavenly suit with a fur collar and hat to match. Mink. Her hands on the wheel would have pink nails. No they wouldn't. At least they would but you wouldn't see them. They'd be under a pair of those lovely sexy string driving gloves with holes on the back. I'd be sitting beside her, my long hair blowing. I'd be in very expensive faded jeans with patches in them and a slinky tee shirt and over the top a great big leathery coat with floating tattery sheepskin down the seams and inside. Our profiles, identical as we sped along, would be very fine.

"I hope it won't be too much of a bore, darling."

"Oh no. I expect I'll get through."

"He's a good-looking boy."

"Hmmmm."

"He's probably out of his mind in love with you."

"D'you think so?" (nonchalant)

"Oh, *clearly*."

We laugh. "*Poor* Jack Rose," she says, "You must let him down lightly."

I leaned my head on the window considering these mothers who never were. I was probably going a little mad again I thought. I didn't really like either of these women at all. Or either of the daughters. It was just – I thought of the profiles again, the smooth-running car, the clothes. The Marigold profile turned slowly to the Grace profile. "I wish I were Grace," I thought. I wish I were with the sort of people Grace is used to. I wish I were sophisticated and cool.

"Cool," I thought and shivered. I was cool enough anyway today. I was absolutely frozen in the bus – except down my right-hand side where this great warm weight was. I looked round – the conductor was coming for tickets. The woman next to me was the woman I'd seen stuck in the kiosk in the pier, the woman so fat that when she fell down she couldn't get up again.

She swelled and bulged all over the seat and wheezed and heaved about. On her knee was a great big dirty-looking bag with a zip-fastener on it and she was burrowing about in it. She took out a great meat sandwich and began to eat it, putting it down on the zip as she felt down in her pocket for her purse as the conductor paused beside us.

"Marston Bungalow," I said and got my ticket.

"Marston Bungalow," said she.

Chapter 14

"YOU GOING TO Marston Bungalow then?" she said, taking an ample bite of the sandwich. "It's a good way but it's worth it when you get there. There's grand places round about. D'you live round there?"

"No."

"Visiting?"

"Yes."

"I been visiting. Down Marske way. I been visiting me daughter. She works on the pier. It's a nice little job but it's a bit slow. You been to the pier?"

"Er – yes."

"Lovely dances. There was a real class dance there one Saturday night. Evening dress. Mind you I like ordinary dances best. Eeeeh – laugh. They're that wild. Sometimes you'd think they'd knock the whole place down. And drink – eeh, dear me. There was some of them – at that class dance, too – that drunk they broke off a whole great bit of the pier and threw it int' sea. The police'll be after them my daughter says. Oh she sees a bit of life in the kiosk now and then. I sit with her sometimes but it gets close. Sometimes I go to the Bingo. Do you go to the Bingo?"

"No."

"D'you live there, then – Marske way? Warrenby way?"

"Yes."

"And you've never been to the Bingo. Eeeh dear! How long

you staying at Marston Bungalow?"

"I'm not staying. I'm going on."

"That's nice. Where to?"

"I'm going to a doctor's."

"Oh dear," she looked very interested, "Would you like a sandwich?" Another sandwich with beef flapping out of the bread emerged.

"Oh – no thanks."

She munched.

"In trouble?"

"Trouble?"

"Seeing a doctor."

"Oh – oh no."

"I just wondered.

"You just seemed," she said after some time, "a bit worried like, it seemed to me. A bit upset." Into her bag went her not very clean hand again and came out holding a huge banana. "If you *was* in trouble," she said, "you just come and see me. I'm not that far from Marston Bungalow. I'm at Marston Hall. You can't miss it. I'm Mrs Deering."

I thought not in a million years, not for fire, flood, pestilence or famine would I go near such a person as you ever, ever, ever. Turning away from her I pretended to look out of the window and when we got to Marston Bungalow I let her ease her way sideways down the bus, scream a greeting or two to one and another about her, blare out a goodbye to the conductor, stand and wave to me vaguely on the pavement. Then I got out.

I caught another bus to Middlesbrough and another one to Ironstoneside West. It was very easy. By the time I had negotiated that last bus I was feeling more alert and pleased with life. The passengers were all "men at the works" or shopping ladies and made cracks among themselves in loud hard Teesside voices. They tried to draw me into the talk and laugh too and I wished I could have joined in very much but not being used to it I couldn't. I kept on blushing and pretending to read a book. "Ironstoneside Road," called the girl, "Here's yer stop, luv," and out I got, frozen stiff but feeling that time and the hour wears out the longest day and whatever they were like the Roses couldn't actually destroy me.

"It is *exactly* by the bus stop. Exactly," father had told me Mrs Rose's voice had said on the phone. "Tell her when she gets out in front of her is number 16. It is just *there*."

Funny thing was that it wasn't.

Number 16 was there but it wasn't a doctor's. There was no doubt about that at all. It was a dentist's — a very definite dentist's. Over the front door — it was a detached house with a semi-circular asphalt drive — was a big white glass cube, the sort that lights up at night and had DENTIST printed on it in black letters.

I wondered what to do. I looked at the houses on either side behind their semi-circular drives but they didn't say anything about being doctors. I walked back and looked at the first one. Number 16 all right. I went up the drive. There were two brown plaques one on each side of the door. One said Janice Rose, B.D.S. (Lond.) and the other Humphrey Rose, B.D.S. (Lond.). On each side of the door there was also a brass bell. Above the door were two windows side by side with a joint black balcony, all curlicues. The house was made of white lavatory brick and on either side of the front door was an identical mustard-coloured conifer. Two ever-mustards. The symmetry of everything was so marked that one felt there was a mirror about somewhere, a very cheap, clear mirror without powers of enhancement and there was a deadness and silence over the house that added to the unreality. I had never seen a building that struck such a chill.

Perhaps, I thought as I climbed the steps and stood wondering which bell to press, it is something in the atmosphere. When you think of it, all the people standing here on these steps, hundreds and hundreds of them, every half hour, six days a week, sweating and praying, "Oh God please don't let there be anything the matter. It's quite stopped hurting now. Please let it only be a scrape and polish" — it's bound to make a difference to a place.

But I'm supposed to be a mathematician, I thought. Why do I suppose anything of the sort. Atmosphere! Really! And anyway, what about all of them coming out. It's quite nice seeing people springing out of a dentist's, all smiles. It's over! Another six months. Whoopee!

Dentists are among the benefactors, the restorers to sanity,

114

they're marvellous people, dentists. You keep your dentist for years. You travel miles to get back to him again. Uncle Edmund got in an awful fit when his died in the Isle of Wight. Like homing salmon they are, patients of dentists following almost unfelt tingles, twinges and pangs, crossing oceans, crossing mountains, up the rapids, dentistwards.

There's nothing *wrong* with dentists. It was just that I'd been thinking of this country house.

I pressed the bell — Mrs Rose's — and a girl in a white coat, nipped in at the waist with a stiff belt, appeared with a pad and pencil and half-moon eye-brows and said, "Yes?"

"I'm Marigold Green."

"Green?" She consulted the pad, "We haven't got you down. Is it *Mr* Rose?"

"No. It's — " I felt myself going heavy and solid and glowery. "It's Jack Rose."

"*Jack* Rose. I'm afraid there's some mistake. Just a minute." She shut the door firmly and then came back with a second appointments book. "Could I come in?" I asked. "It's a bit cold." She didn't look very keen but I picked up my suitcase and stomped by. "I'm sorry," she said in a high voice which tried to sound a bit better than Ironstoneside, "you'll have to wait. There's some mistake."

Just then, like one of those weather toys gone wrong, a door on the left of the hall and a door on the right flew open and two dentists sprang out, each holding a silver spike and dressed in long white coats and masks like gangsters.

The female dentist just stared.

They were very authoritative people. The surgery behind the female dentist was silent but from behind the male dentist came a scuffling, spitting sound.

A great question mark hung on the air.

"There are no more appointments today," said the male dentist firmly.

"I'm Marigold Green," I said back.

"Oh God! I'd forgotten," said the female dentist. "Hang on." She disappeared. The male dentist said, "See to this will you, Phyllis," and disappeared, too. The receptionist and I stood looking at each other with no enthusiasm whatsoever.

I had arrived at the Roses and it was not going to be much fun.

Chapter 15

BEHIND MRS ROSE's surgery there was a waiting room and behind this along the back of the house a sitting room and there I was led and left and stood with my suitcase beside me for what seemed a great time. Then, at last there was a faint clicking of doors and a released sort of voice saying thank you and goodbye, the shutting of the half-glazed Victorian vestibule door and then Mrs Rose was upon me, drying her hands vigorously on a very clean towel.

"Sorry about that," she said briskly, getting the towel well down into the cuticles. "Silly of me. Thought you were coming with Jack."

"Oh – I thought father had said – "

"He did. He did. I was mixing you up."

She was a biggish woman and there was something of Jack about her manner. Her face was not at all like his – pop eyes, yellow perm, round pouting lips rather spluttery – but something in the set of the shoulders suggested that she would make a useful three-quarter. "Glad to see you," she said. "Glad you could make it. Play golf?"

"Oh – er. No I don't."

"Pity. Thinking of what to do with you tomorrow."

"Oh – er – that's all right."

"What do you usually do on Sundays?"

(Church. Chess. Talk to Paula. Read. Stroke the cats.) "Oh, nothing much."

117

"Oh. Well. Never mind." She looked quickly round for a clock. "Quarter to six. Jack home soon. Like to go up?"

"Er – up?"

"Unpack? Then drink or something?"

(*Had* she known my mother? Could she have known my mother?)

"Oh – yes. I'd like to unpack."

We both looked unhopefully at the small bag at my feet. It wouldn't take long.

Then the door burst open and in came the male dentist. He was without his uniform and had presumably finished with his towel because he advanced on me with big pink dry hands. "Hello there," he cried. "Sorry for the welcome. Mind on other things. Nasty wisdom job. Flaps infected. Two more to come out Monday. Interesting roots. What about a dry martini?"

"Er – hum – her – " I said.

"Marianne – it is Marianne isn't it? – is just going to unpack," said Mrs Rose. "I'm going to change." (So they did change, just like Dorset.) – "I'll take you up shall I? Or can you find your way? Left hand side over the front door."

"Oh – yes. Of course. I'll find it," I said and scurried out.

"*That's* fine," said Mrs Rose.

I went out and stood in the hall. The half-moon eye-brows had gone and both surgery doors were shut. On the hall table was a box for the Dentists' Benevolent Fund. On the walls were many large framed notices saying how well Mr and Mrs Rose had done at college. On a shelf up near the ceiling were ranged about half a million silver cups saying how well Mr and Mrs Rose had done at tennis, hockey, rugger, lacrosse, running and swimming, and two huge oars showed how good Mr Rose had been at rowing. The carpet was of very good quality and covered every bit of the floor and the stair-carpets and wallpapers and landing curtains were tremendously thick and all absolutely colourless – or perhaps fawn mixed faintly with grey. The hall-stand had a little metal tray in the bottom to catch drips from patients' umbrellas and at the foot of the stairs there was a gigantic and terrible china tree trunk with china lichens on it and growing out of it was a fearsome and watchful leather-leaved plant. It looked as if it had been put there to tangle with patients who tried to escape, and I passed it by respectfully as I made for the upstairs. And as I did so I heard from behind from the two relaxing dentists a bark of a laugh. "God knows," I heard Mr Rose say. "Cheer up. You'll go straight to heaven for inviting her. Jack and the other one'll be here soon."

"The other one?" Who was the other one — oh heavens! Was there going to be somebody else? Why ever had I come? Why *ever* had I come? Who could it be? I thought through the First XV and felt sure most of them would be going home for Half Term. They had all had more than enough of each other, as father said, by Half Term to want to go visiting each other. Must be someone without a decent home, I thought. I wondered if it was Terrapin. I wondered what I'd feel if it was Terrapin — with all the rumours of his dreadful background, it just might be. He was supposed to be terribly poor. I thought of many small events — Jack Rose's hand jerking back Terrapin's obscenity at the dormitory window long ago, Jack Rose laughing at Terrapin at the Boys' Entrance door and telling him that I, Bilgewater, was no longer a child and could read James Joyce. No — it wouldn't be Terrapin. He'd not get an invitation here.

I went into the room on the left facing me on the landing — very plushy. Carpet ten inches thick, wallpaper cream with a grey relation of the plant at the foot of the stairs crawling all over it in bas-relief, a wooden, rather over-shiny bed, mountainous with satin eiderdown (cream) under cream candlewick. Cream bedside light. On the wall at the foot of the bed was a large fawn etching of the head of an airedale.

When I had unpacked my washing things and arranged them on the basin (the flannel didn't look so hot. It was an old one out of Paula's lost-property box) I put my spare pants and tights away in a drawer and looked round again. Wardrobe. Dressing-table. No books. It seemed early to be going down again. Passing quickly by the long mirror so that I saw only the merest suggestion of the ginger zig-zags, I went over to the french windows and out on to the balcony and stood there for a bit looking at the lights of distant Middlesbrough, for Ironstoneside was on a rise — a very superior neighbourhood. I'd been told that. That's why I had imagined the country — a sort of park-land and a terrace with stone jars. I hadn't imagined this square light over the door now just beneath my feet, with Dentist on it whose electric wire looped across the balcony and divided my room from the one next door.

As I stood there – and it was freezing cold – this light suddenly blazed out, lighting me up and the rooms behind me. I hoped it wouldn't stay on all night. And then, not exactly thinking what I was doing I stepped over the wire and took a look into the room next door along the balcony.

It was shadowy and I poked the french window with a finger and surprisingly it opened. I stepped in and saw a room identical to my own – cream and sumptuous bed, thick, soft carpet, picture too dark to see what but the same style and size as the airedale and in exactly the same place; wash-hand-basin with very clean glass upside down like mine, wardrobe, dressing-table with little lacy mat. The room was waiting for someone just as mine had been a minute before. It was a twin, but there was a difference, and as I stood there I noticed a lovely sweet romantic smell of summer and saw that on the lacy mat on the dressing-table there was a cut-glass vase and a bunch of flowers – shop flowers, freesias, rose-pink, lavender, dark yellow and white. I'd seen some freesias, in the flower shop at home last week and they were 35p a bunch. There must have been at least two bunches here, and some asparagus fern as well.

I stepped quickly out of the room again feeling worse than I'd felt yet because the flowers told me two things – (1) that the other guest was more important than me (which didn't matter) but also (2) that the other guest arriving any minute with Jack was a girl. You wouldn't put out freesias for someone in the Rugger XV. Perhaps it was only some aunt-woman of course. Some cousin or something, I thought, trying to cheer up; but just as I thought it and stepped out back on to the balcony again there was a great swoosh and honk on the drive below and Jack Rose's laugh and by the light of the dentist lamp I saw looking down the top of his handsome head as he leapt out and ran round to the passenger seat.

Slowly I saw two long and perfect legs emerge from this seat, in jeans. Above them came a sheepskin coat, and then, her glorious hair emblazoning the night, came Grace Gathering.

Chapter 16

I LET THE hearty cries of welcome in the hall below subside and sat on my bed for a while after a door had shut leaving a great deal of silence behind it. Then with Paula's clear voice beating in my ears ("Beware of Self Pity." "It is not oneself who is at the centre of things." "To be happy, forget yourself and take an interest in the rest", etc. All that unhelpful stuff) I got up and without a glance in the mirror went down to the sitting room.

I felt Jack there almost without seeing him – his big dark figure handing a glass. Mrs Rose now sitting easily back in a vast sofa, lighting a cigarette and Mr Rose his feet in a heavy rug looking as if the world was a good place behind a glass of gin, his eyes on Grace as if they would never look away. For all three it was obvious, though goodness knows how one realises it just by opening a door and one be-spectacled glance (I'd gone back to the glasses), that the evening for them all had great possibilities.

Grace was draped in a chair, still in her jeans, gazing at the huge electric bars that had been fastened across the old marble fireplace. They were sturdy bars and all switched on and the room had several very efficient-looking radiators, too. I grew damp and prickly under the ginger wool the minute I opened the door for the dress had long sleeves and a high neck and was about three-quarters of an inch thick. Our House is very cold with stone floors meant for monks. You get used to it but you always wear a lot of layers. Not here.

Yet Grace – and the Head's House is no warmer – appeared to be wearing only a long cotton shirt over her jeans, very tight and not even a bra, you could tell, though she was so lovely and thin it didn't matter. The sheepskin was lying all over the back of her chair and her luggage – a sort of canvas nose-bag with a long bit of string – lay on the rose-coloured carpet. "No, just orange," she was saying as I came in and looked up into Jack's face with a slow, sweet smile.

"Bilgie!" cried Jack swinging round, "You're here. That's great. Come on – you have Grace's gin and tonic then," and he thrust a great big cut-glass drink into my hand, about a quarter of a pint of it. "Found your way? Good. Here's to you. We won, Humphrey."

I looked round for someone else and then realised he was talking to his father. "That's the stuff," said Mr Rose. "Let's have another to celebrate." He helped himself. "Good game?" They began to talk rugger, Mrs Rose joining in. She spoke very knowledgeably, in short bursts, about tries and penalties and conversions. When she wasn't talking she lit cigarettes. The glasses were refilled again and Mr Rose waxed very jolly and going across to get himself another gin bent down and whisked away my glass which I saw was empty. I realised that I was feeling very warm and pleasant inside. I had not drunk gin before, associating it either with night clubs which I had not come across or with the sort of person I had sat next to on the bus.

But it was nice. It was making me grin.

"Bilge is grinning." It was Grace, sipping an orange juice, dropping her eye-lashes. It was the first thing she'd said that acknowledged that I was there. Everyone looked at me and for some reason they all began to laugh, even Grace, throwing her head back and taking in my ginger dress which was getting all steamy under the arms. Jack laughed, too, as if he didn't really want to but couldn't help it. Mrs Rose exploded briefly and Mr Rose boomed. It wasn't quite kind the way they laughed. It was at me not with me or for me.

"That's the stuff," bellowed out Mr Rose passing me another quarter pint. "Drink up folks. Dinner's ready isn't it Janice?"

We all trooped down into the bowels of the house where there was a room full of curious oak furniture with bulbous legs and an oak hatch through which two hands of an unseen servant kept appearing. Messages were called out in loud voices to this servant by both the dentists – messages full of very good will like "Wotcher, Mac," and "This looks like just the job, Mac," "Pretty good nosh, girl. Get plenty yourself," and you could hear the knife and fork of this person through the hatch, munching apart.

There was prawn cocktail, coq-au-vin and a wonderful chocolate pudding or rather collection of chocolate puddings – round éclair things stuffed with cream and smothered in dark chocolate sauce like Sunday House-gravy. Then there was a huge obtuse-angled triangle of soft creamy cheese and there was with all the courses a lot of wine and I had some of each kind, after drinking the second glass full of gin in a bit of a hurry before we came down.

I didn't know that there even existed food like this and I ate and ate. I wondered whatever Paula and father would make of it. I wondered how poor Jack Rose managed on our House food at school. I kept on drinking but my glass always seemed to be full and Mr Rose and Jack walking round and round the table with more bottles. Dimly, as the evening wore on I perceived Grace, cool, silent, beautiful, leaning back with tiny teaspoonfuls of food on her plate, not bothering with it much, or relaxed watching, smoking a cigarette. Mrs Rose was now red and shiny in the face, Jack had a really rather silly look on his and Mr Rose looking like something that has been boiled for hours and turned into scarlet rubber.

"Do ourselves well here," he cried. "No surgery tomorrow. No night work for dentists so they can live it up all their lives of a Saturday night. Eh Jack? Not the same for doctors. Doctors can't let up. You take the chance of a good time while you can get it, boy. You've only got six years left. Once you're out of medical school you'll have to stick the toffee on your nose."

Everyone thought this dreadfully funny and I heard myself laughing like mad.

"Liqueurs," called Mr Rose. "Crème-de-menthe anyone? Come on Bilgewater – may I call you Bilgewater?"

I looked thoughtfully at the thimbleful of beautiful green liquid.

"I believe she will," laughed Jack heartily and catching his glance I saw again, even through the haze and the queer tilt of the table, how remarkably small his eyes were, and how careful; and I knew that he had completely forgotten that he'd kissed me last Saturday week on the pier.

"No thanks," I said, "I think I'll go now."

"Go? Not home I hope?" laughed Mrs Rose. "Just as we've got to know you."

I was at the door holding hard to the door handle. I couldn't quite think where I did want to go.

"Ten o'clock news?" suggested Mrs Rose, which sent them into paroxysms of mirth.

Then Grace was mysteriously beside me hitching her canvas bag on to her shoulder and piloting me through the door. Nonchalant and confident as a pale giraffe she called over her shoulder, "D'you mind? I think it's bedtime. Goodnight."

"Which is your room?" I heard her saying. Then all I can remember is sinking or rather having been somehow deep sunk in the cream bed, the light from the square lamp outside lighting up the vegetatious wall paper, the head of the airedale revolving slowly in terrible tilting semi-circles as the bed swooped and tossed on a silent demonic sea.

Chapter 17

I AWOKE TO the knowledge that something was horribly wrong and trying to lift my head off the pillow remembered what it was. The bed had stopped tipping about. The dawn was breaking, the light outside had been put out as the winter sky lightened faintly, yellowly over Middlesbrough. Beyond the balcony I saw the noble face of Paula and the bewildered face of father gazing at me from the clouds and I felt saturated in most terrible guilt. Then all went blank again and when I next opened my eyes, carefully, one at a time, it was daylight.

I felt better and got up and went creeping out on to the landing to find a bathroom. There was a shell pink one with a pink, hairy fitted carpet made of loops and a battery of gilded taps and showers. I took off my pyjamas and had a steaming noisy and gigantic bath. Then back in the pyjamas I marched and climbed into bed and slept a bit more.

When I woke up for the third time I felt quite different and sprang out of bed, brushed my hair like mad, got into my clothes and pranced down the stairs. The clock in the hall said ten forty-five, but there was silence on every side. I went on downstairs to look for the dining room where there was a smell rather like in the foyer of the pier ballroom, but the table was laid for breakfast and had a packet of cornflakes on it. I helped myself to a large bowlful of them and still feeling pretty good looked round for what to do next. There was some bread on the bulbous sideboard and I ate several slices of it and a lot of butter and marmalade that were on the table. Then I looked through the hatch into the kitchen but the serf person didn't seem to be there. There was an electric kettle however and a jar of instant coffee and I felt that more than anything in the world this was what I wanted.

But how could I get at it? I went out to the passage and couldn't seem to see any kitchen door. I went back to the dining room and could only see a door into a cupboard. There was still a very thick and oppressive silence everywhere and the hatch was large, so, carefully moving a magnificent electric hot-plate to one side I began to climb slowly and cautiously head-first through the hatch.

There was nothing to it. It was not high. It only needed the smallest upward jump, and yanking myself on to the sill I caught hold of the shelf on the other side to drag myself through, expecting at any horrible moment to hear the door behind me open and Mr or Mrs Rose cry out with embarrassment or amusement at my receding knickers. I will *never* drink again, I thought.

I fastened my eyes steadfastly on the coffee and the distant draining board: and then beyond me in the kitchen which was very untidy and messy I saw Jack and Grace rolling about together in silence on the floor.

They didn't see me.

I went to church.

Father and I have always gone to church on Sunday and Paula to her chapel. Father and I don't go to the school service at the parish church where the boarders go, but to a church labelled "High" at the end of the town where there is the Sung Eucharist every week at eleven o'clock with a difficult sermon, the Kyrie in Greek and a good long row of lovely candles on the altar which has a cloth of gold altar-frontal at festivals.

It has never occurred to me not to go to church and I was confirmed with almost no instruction, the priest being a friend of father's who said I was a safe bet for a Christian, being father's daughter. It has worked well. I haven't been to many churches — Scarborough, Whitby, a bleak tin-hut place at Hinderwell one week-end when we tried to have a holiday but didn't stay long. Mathematics has not got in the way of faith.

But I suppose father or someone might have mentioned the fact, reminded me that this, almost the first week-end away from him in my life, would include a Sunday and Church, and what had I thought of doing about it. It had not even remotely occurred to me, for while mathematics had not got in the way of faith, Jack Rose had.

Yet upon seeing Jack Rose and Grace's great big bodies all wrapped round each other on his parents' kitchen floor as I balanced on the serving hatch, something took hold of me tightly which I suppose a mediaevalist would call a Discipline. Forgetting the coffee I wriggled myself backwards, went upstairs, put on my coat, found a ten p. piece and made for the front door. I had not the faintest idea where the church was in Ironstoneside but I set out. There was a pad and pencil beside the box for the Dentists' Benevolent and on the pad I kindly wrote "Gone to church. M. Green," before I stepped out into the street.

The Roses' terrace was on the edge of a block of terraces all Victorian and quiet, with linings to the curtains and edges kept very straight around the lawns. I tramped about these terraces a while then down the hill into red-brick country, a black railway bridge, a terrible dingy hospital with iron gates, and up a rise again towards the clanging of a deadened bell to a massive church whose grimy west door built about 1840 might have let through a double decker bus.

A vast and vaulted icy cave smelling strongly of paraffin was within. Red-roped, all the pews until you got to within ten pews of the fumed oak rood screen were looped off. In these ten long pews about fifteen old ladies sat and inside the rood screen were about seven more dressed in black cassocks and mortar boards like Uncle Edmund's. These, with belligerent faces all turned in my direction (because I was late – it was quite ten past eleven) were informing the Lord of their regret at having sinned in thought word and deed and in what they had left undone.

The church was freezing. The two paraffin heaters wilted and waned beneath the might of the thirty-foot pillars. There were a few electric lights on long strings, two candles on the altar unlit, and an organ which when it at length drew difficult breath was like a sigh upon a cold east wind. I knelt down for a minute on a hassock that crackled and had a tuft growing out of a corner. The other members of the congregation were leaning deeply over the pews and did not stir. The vicar as he approached the lectern for the epistle looked briefly and without interest at me and his voice was small and faded away quickly into the spent spaces above his head.

The Gospel and the sermon must have come and gone, the Prayer of Humble Access, the Comfortable Words. I sat on unnoticing. The fifteen old ladies and I tottered to the altar and took Communion and tottered down again. I felt that great wafts of alcohol from the night before still surrounded me and when one of the old ladies staggered on the chancel steps I thought for a moment that she had been overcome by them. At the Gloria I thought the vicar eyed me. He had spotted an alcoholic and he planned to speak to me later at the church door.

Yet all these surface anxieties flowed and floated along, hardly touching the immense preoccupation that swam beneath the wave. All the time, oblivious to the words on my lips which kept them I suppose somehow on the move, I was thinking of Grace and Jack. I was remembering Grace at the pier, and Jack in the park. I was thinking how easy it would have been for Grace to have told me she had been invited, too — how easy for her, knowing — because I was sure that she knew somehow what I felt about Jack — how easy for her with all her conquests, legendary in the past and their absolute certainty in the future, to have left me Jack for just this one week-end. Jack whom I had known and loved so long.

And remembering her dreamy face, I knew that I had been a fool from the start not to see in it the necessity for its universal victory, its thrust for homage and conquest. When we got at last to the Blessing I began to see Grace not even as a human being at all. She was a siren. A water-sprite, Ondine the enemy, cold, uncaring, much beloved.

The choir had filed out, the fifteen old ladies limped off, nodding, depositing hymn books on the font and the organ had fallen into the wheeze that precedes sleep when the vicar emerged from the priest's vestry in a dreary fawn overcoat and clattered towards the chancel steps to turn down the paraffin heaters: but still I sat on.

The paraffin heaters squeaked a bit as he turned the wheel first of one and then the other, and straightening up he said, "Ah. Hullo? Want to see me? Cold day."

I glowered across.

"No good putting them right out yet. Not till after Evensong. Though we might all go into the chancel for Evensong. Never more than six."

His voice echoed round the enormous empty church. He came up to me and stood looking down. "New here?" he said. "Afraid there's not much here for the young. Very few young people."

I still said nothing.

"Are you in some sort of trouble?"

I said no, in a funny voice. I hadn't spoken since last night and I wondered if it sounded ginny. I wondered if he'd think – he might spot that I was –

"I've just got a hang-over," I said.

"Oh dear," he said. "what did you drink?"

"A lot of gin and wine. About half a pint of gin."

"Are you in trouble?"

"No. At least – "

"Why not come back to the vicarage. There's not much. My housekeeper's hopeless but there'll be some beefburgers or something. Plastic frozen peas. And beer," he said, "I like beer. Beer might cheer you up."

"I don't think it would," I said.

"You far from home?"

"Yes. Very far," I said, "I'd better go now though. I'm supposed not to be here. I'm staying with some people. But thank you. Thank you very much indeed."

"Don't mention it. I'm sorry. We like a bit of company. I rather seem to waste Sunday afternoons. Big trial of faith this place."

I looked at him for the first time. His weary face had kind eyes. His hair was white and thin. He was wearing grey woollen gloves like a small schoolboy's. "Never mind," he said, "Christmas is coming. Are you staying with these people long? Are they nice people?"

"No I'm not," I said, "and they're not. They're not nice people at all. They are probably the most awful people I have ever met."

"Well pray for them," he said, "And so shall I. And for you," he said, waddling off.

I walked slowly, slowly up the road again, under the railway, past the hospital, slowly away from the grit and the grime of the old town and up the hill towards the Roses' house again. A fat lot of use that'll be, I thought. You can't pray for my trouble. Infatuation, it's called. Being in love. Christianity is supposed to be all about love but it's utterly useless when you're *in* love. There's not a blind thing you can do about being in love it seems to me except sit it out. Jesus said love one another. He said the only commandments that matter are to love God and each other. He didn't say that loving, especially each other, tears you to pieces. Might have been better if he had said *Don't* love one another. Just try and get along with each other and if you feel love coming on go for a long brisk walk like father tells Uncle Edmund.

The trouble with me is, I thought staring again at the pitiless mirror-front of the double-dental villas, "The trouble with me is," I snarled, thinking of the horrors within and how I detested them all, "is that I've loved people far too much. But not any more. I'm finished with love. I've finished with men. And I've finished with friends."

Chapter 18

A GREAT PARTY was going on when I re-entered the house and the noise of it was all over the ground floor. You would not have believed that so much could have happened in an hour and a half. I had left a house of the dead, the morning after the night before, a house scarce able to lift its lids. I returned to shouts of laughter, a haze of cigarette smoke, the clink of glasses. About fifteen to twenty people were in the living room – about the same number as had been at church – but these were painted and ear-ringed and collared and brilliant-tied and talking very loudly over each other's heads.

I slunk in among them and stood by the door unnoticed by anybody until Mrs Rose materialised from somewhere in natural wool and high heels and said, "Oh good – there you are. Come and meet some people," and I was presented to a man with very watery eyes talking about Harold Wilson and a man in a navy blue blazer and brass buttons talking about bringing back hanging. After a while I drifted elsewhere and someone put a glass of drink in my hand which I looked at very thoughtfully and listened to a woman with a high voice talking about the nationalities of the world. The Irish were dirty, the Spanish were lazy, the French were conceited, the Germans were hard-working but you couldn't help *remembering*. The Swiss were greedy and the Swedes, Danes and Norwegians expected to go to bed with your husband.

"But not if they're *men*," I couldn't help saying and the woman who was talking to another one very like her with the same hard, fortyish stare and little fine pencil lines in a row going downwards from the nose along her upper lip, through keeping it stiff – the two of them turned on me and took me in. "I don't know that there *are* any au pair men," said one of them. The other one said, "I say what super beads," (they were my mother's) and then they both turned away.

People began to shriek off about half past one, the last – the man bent on hanging – ho-hoing about the hall after all the rest.

The Roses and I and Jack eventually achieved the bulbous dining room where ham and salad and mayonnaise and a few of the left over chocolate things in gravy were on the sideboard at about two o'clock. "Hope this suits," said Mrs Rose. "It's always cold on Sundays."

"I thought it always rained on Sundays," said Jack and they all began to laugh uproariously. "It always rains on Sundays," sang Mr Rose. "It never rains but it pours," sang Mrs Rose. "Pussy, pussy paws," said Mr Rose making a gallant sort of lunge at his wife who gave a coquettish little squeak, curious in a useful three-quarter, and dabbed him with her mayonnaise.

"That'll do you two," said Jack and gave me a wink. "Drunk out of their minds," he said. "Are you shocked?"

"Now that'll do, Jack," giggled his mother. "Don't be silly. We're just having a good time. Bilgewater's having a good time too, aren't you?"

"Where's Bilgewater's glass?" Mr Rose approached with yet another bottle. "She's no puritan, I'll be bound. Knew her mother. Where's the other lovely? What you done with the pretty one, eh Jack?"

"Oh – she's fine." He leaned back with a really vast breadth of face and his lip gave a funny curl. I had to look at him. All the time. I simply could not believe it was the same boy as the one who had carried home my books. "She's in bed," he said. "Tired. Sent apols."

"Bit of all right," said Mr Rose crashing his professional teeth on lettuce. "Quite a dish. Hey Janice, wasn't it her mother – ?"

"No, Bilgie's," said Mrs Rose. "I knew her at school."

"Did you?" I heard my voice break in, "Did you *really*?" I

sounded considerably harsher and colder than I had expected – or perhaps it was just because of the general merry rout.

Mrs Rose got up and started pushing plates and dishes through the serving hatch where they were seized by the mystic fingers but not successfully because there was the most almighty crash.

"What-hell?" gobbled Mr Rose. "Hey Jan! Take it easy! You've had too much."

"Oh shut up." She looked red again like last night and flustered. She turned to me and said, "I did know her a bit. She was – " then stopped.

"Did you know her for long?" I said.

"She was – awfully shy," said Mrs Rose.

"Aw, come on now!" Mr Rose had not been following. In fact he had not even started out. He was still mopping up the mayonnaise which was Heinz though in a silver dish, with his bread. "Come on folks. Time for some shut eye."

Shouting and laughing they all made for the door. Mrs Rose took a quick look at the post-drinks-party sitting room and said "Oh God! Leave it for Mac," and one by one the three of them went off to their rooms: and I went off to mine.

Grace's room door alongside was firmly shut. I opened and shut my own door and sat down upon my bed.

I sat there for two hours and I did not stir.

The winter day darkened and still I sat on until I was only a shadow of myself in the glass and the french window turned from grey to dark blue, and at length to black.

I had never seen people drunk before. Not in their homes. I didn't know there *were* houses like this – middle-aged and old people pouring glass after glass of alcohol down their throats till they got silly enough not to know what they were saying nor yet to care. Till they grew oblivious to the other people round them, deluded into thinking of them as eager receptacles of their wit and wisdom.

And Jack so drunk. And enjoying it. And such a fool. Looking such a fool with little spluttery bits of saliva coming out of his mouth like Miss Bex, and that look as if he was trying to control huge indigestion all the time. Parties.

So these were parties.

Though the gin had actually been very nice.

The light came on outside the window and stiffly I got up and drew the curtains and without doing my hair or anything I went downstairs and stood in the hall like a ship awash. Then I went into the sitting room where Mrs Rose was down again and with only a hint of redness round the neck. The friend of my mother.

"Hullo," she said, "Kills you doesn't it? These festivities! God knows how we all get through Christmas. Hardly December yet. Still — have to keep going."

There were sounds off. The rest were coming.

"Mrs Rose," I said, "My mother — "

She opened her mouth and shut it and leaned over the electric fire and began switching every bit of it on — three switches. You could see the struggle going on inside her — trying to say something serious.

"I liked your mother," she said, "Funny — you do remember people from school. Odd the people you know. At school."

"Yes — I suppose so. It's luck I suppose."

"Oh no — not at all," she said, surprisingly definite.

"Those were her beads," she said.

Mr Rose came in, now jacketless with a little scarf tucked into his shirt collar like a pirate his face very genial and unpiratical above. Grace slid in behind him. I saw that Jack who followed quickly put his hand in the small of her back and then moved away.

"Bridge?" cried Mr Rose rubbing his hands, "Oh hell — five."

"That's all right," I said, "I can't play."

"Oh shame. What about Miss England here?"

"All right," said Grace.

"Let's teach Bilgewater," said Jack vaguely.

"Oh — no thanks. I'll watch."

"Telly if you want," said Mrs Rose. "There's one in the waiting room."

But I just sat.

A ferocity began to fill the room and a dreadful silence as different from the silence in chess as tennis from kung-fu, or rather kung-fu from tennis. After about twenty minutes I stood up but nobody noticed. "I think I'll just – " I said.

"ssssh."

A terrible look passed between Mr and Mrs Rose at something Mr Rose had done.

"I'll just – " I tried again when there was a general letting out of breath and easing about and an Over or something seemed to be taking place, "I'll just go and get my book – "

Nobody took the slightest notice – Grace and Jack totally absorbed, though I saw that Jack's foot touched Grace's all the time under the card table.

"Excuse me," I said and went upstairs and packed Paula's suitcase, put on my coat, put my purse in my pocket and went down the stairs again. At the bottom I dropped mother's amber beads with a clatter into the china jar in which stood the all-knowing potted plant. I heard a noise from the sitting room and Mr Rose open the door and say something about getting more tonic, so I picked up the suit-case and went back to my room again, locked the door behind me, turned off the light and stepped out of the french window and dropped the suitcase over the balcony into the drive where it landed with a plop.

I climbed over the balcony and lowered myself down the other side of it until I hung looking inwards, regarding my room from floor level. Then – and it was not easy – I moved my hands down the iron bars bit by bit until my head was on balcony floor level, my body, legs and feet hanging down in space. It occurred to me that if anybody came along the road they would be much diverted. I was clearly to be seen in the light of the lamp which was shining very hot near my left cheek. I wondered if the blue-blazered gentleman were he to come along the road trying to walk off the lunch time festival might think it was a hanging and put up a cheer. It also occurred to me that somebody might just possibly come out of the front door; perhaps to go and look for an off-licence to get more tonic water and opening it be confronted by my feet and legs stirring and swinging in space upon the winter wind. Perceptibly I began to see a face – my mother's – saying "Marigold! Marigold! Whatever next." But then I shut my eyes, let go and fell heavily into one of the mustard-coloured shrubs splaying it outwards so that its twin across the way would never look it in the face again.

"I'm off," I told the pair of them. "I'm off. I've had enough," and I marched out of the gate without the slightest idea what was going to happen next.

Chapter 19

A BUS WAS coming. It was spluttering its way up the hill and stopped outside the dentists' at the stop across the road from the one at which I had got off yesterday. I ran across and stood for a brief moment looking in. There seemed to be nobody on it.

I looked down the hill. I think I wondered for a minute whether to go and see the vicar. Then a voice from the upstairs of the bus called "If you're gettin' on, *get* on," and pinged the bell: so I jumped on and tugged Paula's case up the stairs and went to the very front seat and collapsed on it as the driver gathered speed and jerked vigorously off.

"All the way?" asked the conductor.

"Oh – " I hadn't even seen where we were going.

"Is it Marston Bungalow?" she said.

"Oh yes. All right."

"Twenty-five p."

I opened my purse and there were three ten p. bits. "Oh help," I said.

" 't'sall right. Twenty-five p," she said.

I got my five p. change and wondered what on earth to do. The journey from Marston Bungalow home was as far again. I hadn't brought any more money because I had been expecting to go back with Jack in his car on Monday evening. Paula had said Take Ample. You'll need some for the present for the hostess, but I had thought forty p. – that had included the ten p. at church – would be very much enough.

Oh help.

Oh Hades.

When the bus dragged up to its final abode I got off and found that I was standing at a large and windy roundabout at which very major road works were in progress. There was a huge red notice saying CAUTION HEAVY PLANT CROSSING, a few red lights attached to invisible ropes and the shadows of mountainous heaps of earth here and there in the darkness. I'd noticed on the way out that there did not seem to be any particularly distinguished bungalow at Marston Bungalow: or rather that there were thousands and thousands and thousands of bungalows or little red semi-det villas stretching away as far as I could see in all directions but one, which was the dark line of "the country" which the hungry, hideous city of Teesside was slowly creeping up to, eating nearer bite by bite, the cells of all its little towns floating nearer to each other, then sticking together in an always denser and more nondescript mass – like a disease of the blood. Far away behind the twenty thousand identical streets were the lights of some unloved tower blocks and beyond these a city of fluorescent light, pencil chimneys with small orange paint-brush heads of flame, flares, blazes of fire from furnaces, and wafting smells of gas.

At "The Bungalow" where I stood at the edge of this great dead Sunday city was a shop or two lit up and shut. Through the uncurtained windows of the anonymous street-end nearest me there were the bluish lights of the television sets, and except for myself there was no living creature to be seen.

A wind behind me off the moors, "the country", blew across the roundabout bringing a flurry of sleet with it and I made for the bus shelter whose windows were mostly knocked out. It smelled of lavatories. I stood and held on to the five p. in my hand.

What was Marston Bungalow? Whom did I know at Marston Bungalow? Nobody at my school came from so far, no one at St Wilfrid's came from so near.

There must be a telephone box. I set off skirting the road works putting my head down before the sleet and walked all round the kerb of the roundabout. A sudden car screamed at me as it went by, almost knocking the suitcase out of my hand. Nearly back where

I'd started I saw the phone box and fell into it. It was lightless – the bulb shattered, the smell worse than in the shelter. As another car swished by the broken pane in the side I saw FUCK OFF scratched fiercely on the wooden board beside the instructions panel. I picked the receiver up but though I joggled it and shook it, and pressed hard on the little pegs, it was silent as the night.

Marston Bungalow, I thought. Who lives – and I remembered the terrible woman who had sat next to me and eaten meat sandwiches and found the pier kiosk a bit close. She'd got off at Marston Bungalow. She'd been going to Marston Hall. I'd rather die, I thought, than go looking for her.

It grew very cold in the phone box and I went back to the shelter, turned up my collar and stood with my back to the blast and my hands in my pockets. Marston Hall, I thought.

A bus came bounding out of the night like a lighted palace, its windows steamed up with the warmth. It was not the Middlesbrough bus. It was going to Whitby – miles away. It looked a cheerful bus, packed with people all chatting and laughing and the conductor gave me a welcoming wink.

"Are you gettin' on?" he asked, holding his horses for a moment at the bell.

"Um – is it Marston Hall by any chance?"

"That's right."

"Is it far?"

"Five p."

I got on. It seemed right that I should. I had a distinct feeling as I climbed in that things were being arranged for me. Giving up my five p. and receiving a flimsy ticket back I asked the conductor to tell me when we were there and sat awaiting events to take me into their hands.

But I was nevertheless a little surprised when the bus swung away from the great plain of lights and humanity on to the dark places of the moor. Marston Bungalow was not a bungalow as Marston Chase was not a hunting lodge, nor Brambles Farm had not been a farm since Queen Victoria ruled the waves: and Marston Hall I did not expect to be a Hall, but another "estate" like these. Everybody lived on estates. "We live on the estate," they all said. "Which estate are you on?" Uncle Edmund often talked about this, piping his eye. "They talk like eighteenth-century farm-hands," he said, " 'I am on the estate'. Alas, alas!" Our own town outside the oasis of St Wilfrid's School was a mass of estates, Ings Farm Estate, Marske Hall Estate, Ramshaw's Estate – Ramshaw's had been the farm that father and I used to walk to on Sunday evenings to see the rabbits, now a great warren itself. All the old landmarks were gone – the cricket green, Kirkleatham Hall "where the King stayed" – all flattened to bear the large pink spawn of sameness over the earth. The march of the little houses.

Squeaky violins.

I'd better shut up or I'll be getting like Old Price. "Marston Hall," the conductor called and I got out.

I got out into a blackness and a bitter wind and a lightless road very much blacker than the roundabout and blacker still after the bus had gone. Except for the wind and weather there was utter silence and not a light anywhere in earth or heaven.

The bus had brought me to the moor's edge. It was Sunday and – I couldn't see my watch but I imagined – about eight o'clock. Buses to Whitby are rare at any time and it would be unlikely that there would be another one tonight.

Marston Hall. Whatever it was, I thought looking around, it wasn't an estate. It appeared to be an area of main road without a sign of life upon it. A car whizzed by and a few minutes later another, lighting up the snow in their headlamps.

I leaned back on a sort of post and thought that perhaps the next car I ought to try and stop, but no more cars came. I put my hands between my back and the post to keep it off the cold stone. I thought of Jack Rose's hand in Grace's back.

Cold stone.

I felt along. It was a big stone. I turned round and looked up and saw a sturdy pillar with some large piece of carving on the top of it. To the right I saw another pillar and between them a space. Like the awful shrubs, I thought and then – no. They are not. They are not at all like. I moved along a bit and looked into the darkness between the posts. Then I felt about and there was aged metal, peeling, cold. A great tipped gate. They were the stone posts of a huge gateway leading into blackness: the gates of Marston Hall.

It was a Hall. A real Hall. I picked up the suitcase and, with my left hand out in front of me I began to pick my way like a blind person over bumpy, tufty terrain, between tossing trees into, for all I knew the very pit.

I passed a little building but derelict, unlit – a lodge. The road dipped down and round a bend, then seemed to be going uphill again. I pressed forward in the wind, on and on, and kept stopping and trying to look here and there. Darkness. On and on and trees on either side. I began to think that the road was not really there. All roads must lead or have led to somewhere yet this one had no sign of intention or hope in it of any kind. I could not even see it. It was just the space between two lines of trees. Perhaps it wasn't there.

I was on the top of a rise now. My stockings and shoes were soaked through, my hair sticking cold to my face, my hands frozen. All still dark. There could be no Hall here.

Then I saw over to my left a faint light. It came and went and was at some height from the ground and I thought that perhaps it was some queer low star. Then I realised that it was a light coming and going because it was behind trees that waved and strained and shook themselves in front of it.

The path turned now in the direction of the light. The snow had stopped falling and the wind as I stepped out of the trees blew the blizzard away for a moment letting through the moon. It shone bleakly on the path, a curved, rough driveway with patches of sleet, turning round to the end of a terrace with a low wall of urns and balustrades. The terrace itself when I got on to it was broad and slabbed with great old stones, a forecourt for a castle keep.

The house it belonged to stood up behind, gigantic under the fitful moon, black against a wild white sky. The caverns of its many eyes were dark and uncurtained, the moonlight on the roof showed holes and patches and a great crack tumbled like a suicidal flight of steps down the side of a turret, nearly to the ground, as if with a shove the turret might have been heaved away to fall apart from its parent wall, crash down and vanish like the staircase on the pier. In the turret window at the top there was a light, presumably the one I had seen. Then as I looked I decided that after all it wasn't: it was just a reflection of the moon. The house was a ruin, long ago deserted, waiting for the end.

Marston Bungalow was better than this, I thought. Television sets and lighted chimneys and fumes and ferments: at least that desert had people in it.

There was a great door like a church and church-like pointed windows in the thick rough walls on either side and a long, rusty-feeling bell-rope hung beside the door. I pulled on this not expecting it to move. But it moved easily very far down in my hand until I thought I might be pulling it down altogether. I had the fancy that I was about to pull the whole great house down, that there would be a rumble and a crack and the massive, pathetic old place would slowly subside around my feet. I knew from the utter stillness that it was empty, a house dead long ago waiting for its final destruction.

When I let go of the chain however, it moved smoothly upwards with a long groan and though there was no sound of a bell the house stood on.

The idiocy of it all suddenly hit me as the wind struck up again and the moon disappeared before the next attack of hail and sleet. It frightened me so that it almost made me stumble and fall. I had no idea where I was. I had not one penny. I was soaked to the skin and I had fled the house of two cheerful and hospitable dentists and two good friends, fled from them into space without a word. I was utterly helpless, utterly irresponsible, utterly unwise. I, Bilgewater – I, and I turned away from the unlikely door ready to make off in any direction, anywhere, anywhere, into the night.

With a huge squeal and groan of its hinges the great door, now behind me, was pulled very slowly wide open and Terrapin stood looking at me, an oil lamp held high above his head.

Chapter 20

HE SAID, "I was doing a prose. Come in."

I said, "But I thought you were poor."

We each stood, letting the two statements sink in, letting them hang about for future reference, like memos in a rough note book: like Paula's great pad above her telephone labelled NOTES AND POINTS OF REFERENCE. The oil lamp blazed up and a blast of wind blew me towards him into the hall.

He stood looking at me very seriously indeed, his fair hair hanging down, his cheek-bones gaunt, his eyes round and large and blue. I noticed how tall he was, the immense length of his legs in black velvetish trousers, his long thin top half in a white roll-top jersey and I thought again, he is like a clown. A very distinguished, marvellous clown.

There was something else about him, too, which I found difficult to admit because it was an archaism, a sort of borrowed standard, the sort of thing that my dearest Uncle Edmund HB or silly Puffy Coleman or pathetic Mrs Gathering might have said. He looked a gent.

There. He did. Churning out uranium in a Siberian mine, slopping about in the communist rice-fields of China, marching shoulder to shoulder with the workers, wagging the biggest red flag in the world, sitting in a hole in the road with a hanky round his head knotted greasily at each corner, Tom Terrapin would look a gent. Like Robert Graves said he did, like George Orwell wished he didn't, like Lancelot was and didn't even notice. Tom Terrapin looked the young master, the lord of high estate. I thought of smooth pin-eyed Jack Rose lying back on the pink plush, his voice just a bit near the upholstery, Jack Rose the answer to the maiden's prayer, Jack Rose who didn't live in Shalott after all. I thought, my goodness, I've been getting them the wrong way round.

He said, "Well, how was the country-house week-end?"

I blinked through my dim specs.

"At the Rose establishment? I thought you were off for a couple of days hunting."

"We − didn't," I said.

"It was Bridge," I said. "And drinking. They were dentists. They believe in hanging."

"You're rather wet."

I looked down and saw that I was indeed so wet that a puddle was squashing out of my shoes and surrounding my feet on the filthy marble floor. The floor spread for great distances and like the terrace outside was made of a chessboard though here of vast marble squares. A very battered but beautiful staircase rose up from them some fifty feet away, dividing into two at the top and surrounding the hall as a gallery. There were niches in the staircase wall, some with statues in them and there was a broken column near my elbow with the bust of a Roman nobleman on it, lacking a nose. At the foot of the staircase was a huge motor-bike standing on clean newspaper with bits and pieces of spare-parts and tools around it, very tidily arranged. The place was absolutely freezing, so cold that puffs of white smoke came out of our mouths when we spoke, like arctic dragons.

He said, "How on earth did you get here?" still staring, lowering the lamp so that the shadows darkened under his cheek bones and gave his long narrow nose a haughty look like Sir Walter Raleigh or Mr Chou En Lai; and I felt at once a sort of peasant − and a fool again and wet and silly and ugly, running in from the rain.

"I really only came to speak to a Mrs Deering," I said primly, shivering as my coat clung to me, colder, soggier every moment.

"Mrs Deering! Mrs *Deering*!" He looked absolutely flabbergasted. "Do you *know* Mrs Deering?"

"Yes. She said that if I was in trouble — "

"Are you? Whenever did she say that?"

"I met her. On a bus. She said I looked worried and if I was in any trouble — "

"Mrs *Deering*! She's the housekeeper. She's dreadful."

"I thought she was dreadful. But she said she lived at Marston Hall and I thought it was an estate or a block of flats and I could ask someone. Deering isn't a usual name — " I added feebly.

"But whatever did you want her to do?"

"Lend me the fare home."

"Mrs *Deering*?"

"Yes. I'd got half way. To Marston Bungalow. But I'd run out. I only had five p. left. It was just enough to get here. I didn't know anything about you — so you needn't think — I'd run away. I'd run away from the Roses. It was not possible to stay. They were terrible — terrible. Jack and Grace — "

"Grace was there?"

"Yes."

"Jack had asked her too?"

"Yes."

"Without telling you?"

"Yes."

"The shit."

I began to cry.

"I climbed out of the window," I said through long, horrible sobs, "I dropped from a balcony into a bush. I dropped my mother's beads into a pot. If they are my mother's sort of people they'd better have them. I don't want them. I'm finished with my mother. I'm finished with Jack Rose — waaaaaaaaaaaah," I wailed and Terrapin came over and got me by the elbow and led me howling and bellowing up the Grinling Gibbons, bawling and weeping along the first oak landing, uncaring that Mrs Deering might suddenly emerge from some lair behind the baize nor that the statues of previous Terrapins, scantily draped, were regarding me from their alcoves with expressions of considerable disdain.

"Come on love," said Terrapin hastening me on. "We'd better get you warmed up and sorted out." We marched on up another flight of stairs and along another immense gallery. There seemed to

145

be almost no furniture at all and it was as cold as a museum with the heat turned off in January at the North Pole. Still I wept.

We reached a small door and he pushed me up a spiral staircase in front of him until I burst out of it into a very little round room with slit windows all the way round and a glorious electric fire standing right in the middle. It was the turret room in which I had imagined I had seen the light and there was such a light – an electric bulb hanging on a string down from the inside of the pinnacle. "Take your clothes off," said Terrapin and with a slam of the door was gone.

With the odd, huge sob, but getting odder and further apart, I began unquestioningly to take off my glasses, coat, dress, tights, shoes. There was a towel over a chair and I rubbed my legs with it and hands and hair. There was an iron bed with a red blanket on it very neatly tucked in and I took it off and wound myself in it, wrapping my feet in it, almost covering my head. In the one up-right, kitchen chair I crouched like Old Mother Shipton as close to the fire as I could, hugging myself, giving an occasional great sigh and sob.

Terrapin came back and said, "Good heavens. Here. Put these on," and vanished again, so that after a while I removed the blanket and pulled on the clothes he had tossed through the door. There seemed to be a long black woollen dress with tight sleeves and a queer high neck like someone attending the front row of the French Revolution, and a big fur thing like a hearth mat with sleeves. They had a musty smell about them but the dress was lovely and soft and clung to me all over. The hearth mat was gloriously soft and warm too, and fell about me as if it were almost a living, slinky skin. I sat on the chair and gradually allowed my freezing feet to emerge. I wriggled and stretched my toes to the electric fire.

Then I looked about.

There was a wooden table very cheap-looking, the kitchen chair and the iron bed. On the table were Terrapin's books – a note book, school exercise book, Greek Lexicon and a book of proses open with the pen laid beside it. There was a little box of ink cartridges on the table and an alarm clock with brass bells on top from Woolworths. There was no carpet, no curtaining and the walls were roughly plastered over stone. Behind the door some clothes were hanging – his school suit and his House scarf. There was a wooden chest at the foot of the bed with a glass of water on it, and an apple. That was all. Apart from the electricity which had been permitted to this patch of the house, it might have been a monk's cell, a solitary and enclosed nest which would not have disgraced a hermit or guru. A kingdom of the mind.

Except for an astonishing difference. From the roof of the turret, way above the light, where two beams crossed it, were two rows of hooks, and from each of these, like huge broken flowers hung a company of marionettes. They were big, brilliant, large-handed and shod, with trails and wisps of dresses, flat-trousered, floating-haired. There were asses' heads and sirens and punchinellos and harlequins and señoras with high combs, and ghosts and skulls and witches. There were people I knew. There was a long-necked, bright-cheeked, plume-haired dutch-doll one like Paula. There was a ninny one with loose teeth like Puffy. There was one with a cloud of gold hair and heavy eye-lashes like brushes. They hung there like clusters of bright, dead birds, stirring slightly in the air currents which ran here and there overhead in the upper reaches of the turret like the tide gently rocking the feathery fishes that sleep in the reefs of distant warm seas.

"You look good."

Terrapin had brought a big mug of tinned tomato soup and some bread and butter. "Black," he said.

"What?" I took the mug but still gazed up above my head.

"In black. You look marvellous in black. Black fur, black dress, wet hair. Cheeks aflame. Purple feet."

I put my feet in under the dress. He walked all round me.

"I might make a graven image of you."

"No thanks," I said tearing my eyes away from the heights and drinking the soup. I wondered why I was so happy that he hadn't. I wondered why I didn't feel neglected that I Bilgewater with my frog-face and crude hair and tortoiseshell eyes was not among the rest. "I didn't know you could make things like that."

"You could have known."

"How?"

"You could have known anything about me. We lived under

147

the same roof – just you and I and Paula and your father – for plenty of years.”

I said nothing.

“At first – after the first Half Term I was there all the holidays, too. Wandering about.”

“I was frightened,” I said. “You were on the Other Side.”

“Make me sound like the dead. A shade.”

“Well you hardly *said* anything. You hardly spoke. Didn’t you ever think I might be – well, not used to – ”

“You didn’t exactly chatter yourself.”

I drank the lovely hot soup.

“Thundering about that swimming pool – ”

“You seemed – young,” I said. It was the most extraordinary experience. Wrapped in rolls of black and beauteous furs, feeling the hot bright-orange soup going gloriously down, my very toes responding; the little round room in the tower, the heat flowing up from the fire and making the paper company drift and whisper together above my head – all so strange. And I was speaking truthfully, keeping back nothing, as fearless as if I were talking to myself. But not to myself – to this sweet and most beloved boy. I felt that we knew each other inside out.

He flung himself down on the bed and put his hands behind his head and I leaned forward and looked at the work on the table. I can do Greek. It seemed to be Xenophon. His writing was beautiful – large and very even and sloping and black. I ran my finger over the page and drew up my feet on to the chair-rung.

“Where’re you trying for?”

“Jesus and John’s.”

“Cambridge?”

“Yes.”

“So’m I. Next week like you.”

“Yes, I know.”

“If I get in,” I said. “It’s not so easy for a girl.”

“You’ll get in. You got marvellous A levels.”

I looked over at his profile on the bed. “I didn’t know you knew anything about my A Levels. Anyway, a lot depends on the interview. You often don’t even get an interview if you’re a girl.”

"You'll get an interview."

"How d'you know?"

"Because you're very good."

"My writing's awful. I'm no good at English. The General Paper — "

"English? General paper? I know because I know you. I've known you for years. I've watched you."

"I've known you, too," I said after a time. I put my head down on his work table and let my forehead roll about on Xenophon. Looking up, I thought I saw something that made me uneasy out of the corner of my eye-ball, behind the door, but it was very important, I found, not to concentrate on that. I said, putting my hands over my face for a moment, "Terrapin, I do know you."

"I've lived with you for years," he said.

I said, "Tell me."

"What?"

"Why did you? Why didn't you live here and come in on the bus? Why did you live with us?"

There was a very long pause and the wind howled around outside. The paper creatures swung and fluttered overhead.

"My father went off," he said, "That's all. Nothing so odd. Nothing so unusual. Nothing at all unusual if you'd known my mother. Nothing in the least unusual if you'd known my grandmother."

"Whatever had your *grandmother* — "

"She lived here too. We all lived here. My father had no money. He was a drunk. He was an actor."

"An actor? Here? In Teesside?"

"Yes. He was on the pierrots."

"Whatever are pierrots? I thought they were gnomes."

"They were actors. On the sands. They used to come every summer and put up a tent with an open front for a stage, and rows of deck-chairs and a canvas wall all round. You paid sixpence to come and see the pierrots — in a chair. If you stood round the canvas you saw them free, except that there was a very old pierrot who used to rush round cuffing people and snarling at them to pay or go away. The chairs were nearly always half-empty but there was always a big crowd round the canvas walls."

149

"Why didn't they make the canvas wall higher?"

"No money. They were very old canvas walls anyway. All blotchy and brown and held up with hairy string. The deck-chairs weren't so good either. Neither were the pierrots."

"What are pierrots?"

"Dramatic pre-Christian symbols. Possibly Ancient Greek. They've died out now I think."

Looking at the page of beautifully transcribed prose on the table I said, "You're telling me that your father was a dramatic pre-Christian symbol possibly Ancient Greek?"

"Yep. Old as Punch and Judy. Same roots."

"Terrapin, are you mad? Did you ever *see* your father?"

"Yep. Often. He talked to me. He told me about pierrots and the stage and the drama and the importance, almost the holy importance, of the actor in society. He was long and thin like me. When he was made up he had a black and white costume with a pattern of diamond patches – satin and a white ruff round his neck and a little black hat like a Jew and painted eyebrows and two round red circles painted on his cheeks."

"Did all of them?"

"The pierrots? Yes."

"What did they do?"

"Sing. And dance. And do comic turns. There were pierrot girls, too, in white ballet skirts and black silk bodices. They sang songs like 'When I grow too old to dream' and 'There's a little grey home in the west'. Another pierrot played on an upright piano – with candlesticks sticking out of it, in the background. It wasn't a very good piano – I think the sand had got in it over the years – and when the sea was rough you couldn't hear it very well. And often it was windy, too, and the sand blew everywhere and turned the empty deck-chairs inside out and the audience had to hold on to their hats or put newspapers over their heads. When it rained the audience ran for it and left all the chairs to be gathered and stacked up as fast as possible, and covered with tarpaulins, and the pierrots would stop singing and dancing and go round the back and sit on boxes and drink beer until the rain stopped."

"Did you see them, ever?"

"Yes. Once. My grandmother wouldn't let me for ages. Well,

for ages I didn't know even that my father was one – only that he was some sort of a traveller. I used to get post-cards from him from Torquay and Lytham-St Anne's and Brighton. I think I thought he was a sailor. Then one day he came home – it was when he was doing his fortnight season on the sands round here – and he said, 'Come on, you're coming with me today,' and he took me off on to the sands and sat me in the front row and told me not to move. I was about five I think. I sat there and sat there – it wasn't a very nice day and there were puddles of sea under the chairs. Then after ages the piano began and the curtain went up and there were all these black and white people with red circles on their cheeks and all of their feet in black pumps, stepping and pointing. They sang a song called 'I want to be happy' – very loud, all in a row with their arms round each other's waists. Baritones and contraltos. They were absolutely certain of themselves. I forgot the puddles and the sand stinging my legs and the damp deck chair and I just gazed and gazed. And then very slowly it dawned on me that the most beautiful of the men dancing was my father!"

"Did you – " I said, "Did you – " I was thinking very carefully and feeling very confused. It shows I suppose what a very self-centred life I had had, but the idea of a father step-dancing in black and white satin was so very different from my own – "Did you – *like* it?" (I said it and not him.)

"I – worshipped it," he said. "It was the most beautiful thing that I had ever seen. When the rain really began to come down and the audience went off – some of them throwing pennies and half-pennies into a bag on a stick that the old pierrot who shooed away the gate-crashers held out – when the music stopped my father jumped down off the stage and came over and took my hand and we walked over to the sea in the sea-fret. He went on singing 'I want to be happy' and the wind kept blowing the white organdy ruff into his face and he kept prancing and jumping about."

"It sounds," I said, "as if he *was* happy."

"I think it was just the song," said Terrapin.

"'I want to BE happy
But I can't BE happy
Till I make YOU happy
TOO.'

Actually he had a very tired face under the paint. I do remember that. And I remember how thin the costume was when you were near to it and how cold his hands were. They were blue. He took a brandy bottle out of his pocket and swigged it between the verses."

"Could you – were you old enough to tell him how you loved it – the pierrots?"

"Not really. I don't think so. He did ask me if I knew who he was and I just said 'Daddy'. Then he said, 'I'm Harlequin. I'm called Harlequin and I'm very, very old. Can you say Har-le-quin?' I said Harlequin but I was worried – I don't think I was six – because he'd said he was very old and I said 'Are you going to die soon then?' and he said Never. Never. Never. Never. And did some very crazy sort of dancing by the sea. We'd collected a trail of kids by then even in the rain and one or two dogs. There was an old chap with a white beard who used to go round the sands gathering sea-coal in a cart. And there was a boy with two donkeys. They all stood round and watched my father."

"I'd have died," I said. I couldn't help it.

"What?"

"Well, weren't you – you know – embarrassed?"

"I was so proud of him," said Terrapin, "I was so proud of him he might have been God."

"So what happened?" I said.

"He died."

"But – "

"Well he did. When I was ten. I hadn't seen him for ages. He died at Blackpool of pneumonia. After going on the evening show as usual. We didn't hear for ages."

"But what about your mother?"

"Oh she'd died long before. She never lived with him. She was crazy. She'd got T.B., too – you used to die of it in those days. T.B. makes you very wild and very sexy and you go at things ten to the dozen – like Keats. She was a bit of a terror, my mother. They were in those days anyway – it was the fashion. She was the old-style romantic heroine, my mother. Rode to hounds."

"What?"

"Went hunting. Foxes. On a horse."

152

"What — here?"

"Round here. She lived here — in the Hall. Her family always had done since William the Conqueror. She was a crazy, inbred aristocrat with a curling lip. Two curling lips. She loathed my guts."

"But how on earth — ? How in the world did she meet your father?"

"How d'you think? On the sands. Galloping through the wavelets on her chestnut mare."

"I didn't know there were any foxes on the sands."

He gave me a look. "She was not hunting at that moment. Not foxes. Just romance. She found it."

"Your father? At the pierrots?"

"Right."

"I don't believe it."

"You didn't see my father. I've told you. He was the most marvellous-looking man on earth. I don't suppose he was a drunk then, either."

"And they married? Just like that?"

"Just like that. The nearest altar. It was an utter disaster."

I said, "Oh Terrapin, I'm so sorry." I had got into bed with him by this time. I don't know at which point of the story I had decided to, but there I was. He was still lying with his nose in the air like a knight on a slab but I got up close to him and put my face into his neck. I was very nice and warm now in the long black dress clothes. He felt — his neck and his hands which I'd got hold of — rather cold. After a while he shook my hands off his and scrabbled around and wrapped us both up in the red blanket and we lay there very still.

He said, "No need to be sorry for me now that my grandmother's dead."

"Was she awful, too?"

"My father was not awful."

"I mean was she like your mother?"

"No. She was all right. Just a misery. You couldn't blame her. Her husband had been killed in the First War — he'd been a scholarly sort of gent and they hadn't had much to say to each other. Then mother got TB and married the pierrot and all she'd got left was me."

"But didn't she love you? Did you remind her of the pierrot or something?"

"I don't think so. I just wasn't exactly attractive."

I remembered the gargoyle bellowing about Peeping Toms and the figure with the bulging eyes and croaking throat beside the swimming pool. "You may remember," he said.

I simply surged with love and said, "Oh Terrapin, oh Terrapin. I do so wish she could see you now."

"Now?" he said, "She wouldn't have thought me very promising now. At the moment. In bed with a girl who's wearing her sable coat."

"I'm not in bed with you," I said putting my arms around his neck and feeling tremendously happy that I was, "I mean, not in that sort of way."

"My grandmother would not have distinguished."

"When did she die?"

"Last year."

"It's getting terribly hot," I said, "in this fur coat." We got the coat off somehow under the blanket and chucked it out on the floor. "Anyway, why should she have minded?" I said as we wrapped ourselves up again. "I'm not a pierrot." I was quite enchanted with myself. I had always thought I had very strong views on sexual morality. I found I had nothing of the kind. Perhaps I should have been more carefully Prepared for Confirmation and not just relied on being father's daughter. "I just love you," I said.

After a bit Terrapin said, "Bilge – you ought to watch out with me. I'm pretty unstable."

I said, "Shut up."

"Well, I'm telling you."

"I'm in love with you."

He said, "Look. You ought not to be wearing my grandmother's dress."

"Why not?"

"It gives me the creeps."

"It's a lovely dress."

154

He said, "Take it off."

I found that I said no.

"Take it off," he said more urgently.

There was a string hanging down over the bed for the light so that one could switch it off without getting out of bed and groping for the switch by the door. Terrapin who was not by this time lying like a knight on a slab any more – or not like any knight in any Church that I have ever seen – began to feel about in the air above us to get hold of the string to pull it. At the same moment I got into a panic and somehow or other I got my arm which was half-way out of the granny's dress, free, and began to wave it about in the air, too, trying to catch his and stop him. "TERRAPIN," I said, "Don't." I knew that the light must not go out.

"You fool," he said catching the string. The light went out.

And at the same moment there was a tremendous knocking and thumping on the door of the tower.

Chapter 21

"I've brought you a sandwich," called the voice of Mrs Deering through the door. "Put that light on again. You needn't pretend you're asleep. I saw it go out a second ago round the crack."

"Go to hell," said Terrapin.

"Nice way to talk. And me taking the trouble to come all the way up here with me heart."

"I thought you said it was a sandwich. Don't move," he said into my ear in the dark, "Don't breathe."

"Is it locked?" I whispered.

"No."

"You know what I mean. You know me heart. I'm puffed to death. 'Ere. Let me come in for a sit down. It's stairs does it the doctor says. I feel it on the stairs."

Terrapin called, "It's all right Mrs Deering. I'm not hungry. I'm going to sleep. I've been working."

"Working. Working. Always working – Half Term holidays an' all. Unnatural sort of life. In my day young folks enjoyed theirselves. You ought to be out finding a nice girl."

"Just leave it, Mrs Deering."

"Eh?"

"The sandwich. Just leave it by the door."

"Ont' doorstep? The rats'd get it."

"Don't be ridiculous."

"I'll eat it meself. I like a sandwich."

"OK. That's fine. I got some soup."

"I saw you 'ad. And left t'pan. I saw it when I got in from me Club."

"Sorry."

"Come on now Tom, let us in. Let's have a natter. I been to me daughter's. Dint you 'ear t'car? I thought you'd a bin down when you 'eared t'car."

He said nothing. We were lying side by side now and a good bit apart. The paper people rustled in the dark above our heads.

"All right then," she said. "Just as you like. You've a nasty streak in you Tom Terrapin. So had your Gran. And your Ma — not to mention your Pa if there ever was one. I don't know why I stop on."

"Neither do I," he yelled out back. "You can go to hell."

"Go to hell yourself."

Her footsteps, very slow and creaky and her wheezing breath grew fainter down the turret staircase. In time, a long way off a door slammed.

"I must go now," I said. I swung myself out of bed and felt around for my shoes, got my arm back into the dress. Terrapin found the light string and pulled it and we looked at each other. I began to shiver. He stood by the bed with his hair all in tufts and his eyes bright. His shoes and socks seemed to have disappeared. Quite a lot of his clothes seemed to have disappeared. His feet looked very endearing. Never in my life had I so loved anyone. "I'm going now," I said.

He said, "Bilge — stay. She's gone. She'll not come up again. She won't even see me in the morning. We scarcely meet. She's hardly ever been up here in her life. It was just terrible luck."

I'd got my shoes on and picked up the coat and swathed myself in it. "Please," I said, "Could you take me back? It wasn't just bad luck."

"Why?"

"I don't know. I just have to go."

"So you didn't mean it?"

"I did. I love you."

"Then stay."

"Oh Terrapin, take me back."

"To lovely Daddy Green and Prissy Paula?"

It was then easy. "No," I said quite steadily, "I can't do that. I'm afraid you'll have to get me back to Jack Rose."

"Bilge!"

"I'm afraid so," I said going to the table and putting on my glasses.

"Bilge. I'm sorry. I'm sorry I said that. I like your father and Paula. I owe them a hell of a lot. Look luvvy — stay with me."

"And what are the Roses going to say when I'm not there in the morning?"

"What were they going to say anyway? You weren't thinking of that when you came running to me an hour ago."

"I didn't know you were here. It was Mrs Deering. I had no idea you lived here — I told you. It was co-incidence."

"Bilge do you honestly expect me to believe that?"

"It's true."

"Fate leading you to my door?"

"If you like."

"And Fate in the person of Mrs Deering rescuing your virginity — Mrs Deering messenger of the gods? Mrs Hermes. Mrs Eumenides."

"Shut up."

"You're a coward."

"I'm not. I'm telling the truth. Anyway it's as possible as a father who dresses up in ballet clothes and thinks he's the reincarnation of Punch and Judy."

He said, "We'll go."

His face had gone still. He pulled on his clothes and the coat from the back of the door, wound his House scarf round and round his neck. I pushed my stockings down the front of the dress, fastened up my shoes and buttoned up the sable coat. He opened the door and without even putting out the fire or the light or making the slightest effort to be quiet went clattering ahead of me down the stone stairs. I hovered a minute — switched off the fire, looked all round the room once and saw for the first time clearly what I had seemed to see from the corner of my eye and rejected, soon after I had arrived — Terrapin's latest puppet. It was not yet finished but already very dreadful and good. It was different from the rest —

gross, balloon-like and rubbery with a greedy, ugly, impertinent head; a head so confident and powerful that it held more horrors than anything more ordinarily nasty – any devil or goblin – and it was of course Mrs Deering.

She had been hanging there unfinished in the dark all the time we had been together in bed. Overhead the rest of Terrapin's company swung and whispered in the air the open door was letting in from outside. I shut it quickly and went down towards the sound of Terrapin wheeling out his motor-bike. All the way back through the miserable dark I heard the sound of the puppets laughing and murmuring quietly together.

Chapter 22

IN THE MORNING I woke up to hear Uncle Edmund Hastings-Benson's loud, kind voice in the Roses' hall and I jumped out of bed and saw his massive pre-first-war Rolls Royce standing in their drive. It was still almost dark, but in December it is still dark up to about 9.30 o'clock and this in fact was the time.

I couldn't believe it. I had lain down on the soft cream bed the night before to await the dawn with open eyes. I had lain down in the black dress, vaguely regretting a toothbrush but otherwise in such a curious void and weariness that I would have been hard put to it to utter one word if that had been necessary.

It had been quite unnecessary. Through the night Terrapin's motor-bike had roared with the snowflakes spinning in its headlamps. Behind him I had sat with my arms round his waist, my cheek against his back, his woolly scarf-ends flapping across my snowy glasses. The parts of me that were covered by the sable coat were warm but my hands were so numb that I could hardly cling with them and my feet hanging down under the long dress seemed to have disappeared. We had got to Marston Bungalow in what seemed liked seconds and Terrapin had ignored red lamps, ropes, notices about heavy plants and rubble and bounded over the round-about at huge speed. The lights of Teesside faded away I began to recognise things – Eston lane-ends, the turning for Ironstoneside. He seemed to know exactly where to go.

I began to notice the beginnings of the prosperous terraces all now in darkness with the curtains pulled back for morning – last job of the middle-class day, all the television plugs pulled out.

I began to panic at the thought that we should soon be parting and my heart began to beat so loud that I felt sure he must be able to feel it through our coats. I held tight, and tighter still to him as we turned into the Roses' road – I suppose he must have been there before. Funny – I had thought they were enemies. How little I really knew about the Boys' Side. How little I knew about anyone or anything.

But this didn't bother me – not even the fact that Terrapin must have known all about the Rose ménage when I was boasting about being invited to a grand country-house weekend (Oh God! Oh God! And Terrapin at Marston Hall!) so much as what I was going to say to him when the bike stopped and I had to get off.

For I knew that I had said an unforgiveable thing. About his father. I knew what needed to be said. In a perfect and uncomplicated world where one can say anything without being sneered at or giving offence or being misunderstood I could have said what was right: "Oh Terrapin, I do understand about your father dancing by the sea. I can see how you would love him."

Yet of course this could not possibly be said – or only by a lunatic or a child.

The bike slowed and stopped and Terrapin rested his foot on the ground and waited for me to get off. This was not easy. There was first the long dress and second the disappearance of my feet. In fact as I put my legs upon the pavement they tottered and swayed about and I had to clutch at the pillion and Terrapin's arm.

As soon as I was standing more or less upright he gave an enormous revving to the engine, flung off my hand and paying no attention at all to whatever it was I did say in the end – "Oh Terrapin, I'm so terribly sorry," or something – without a glance in my direction he was off in a flamboyant U turn in the road leaving me very much alone at the end of the gravel semi-circle which was now coated with snow. When the sound of the bike had died away – it took a very long time – there was complete silence as if there was nobody left awake but me in the world.

The Roses' curtains however were not yet drawn back and the dreadful square light above the door was still on, so that I supposed there was a chance that the front door had not been locked yet. I crunched up the drive, swung the door open, remembering my furtive escape from the balcony earlier as the lunacy of the kindergarten, and marched into the hall. There was a light on in one of the consulting rooms – one of the Roses must be preparing for the labours of tomorrow – and, still taking no thought about being seen I went over to the Dentists' Benevolent table and wrote on the memo pad the following message:

Would you be so very kind as to telephone the number below and ask Mr Edmund Hastings-Benson to come and get me as soon as possible.
Yours sincerely,
Marigold D. Green.
(the member of the congregation this a.m.)

I put the number and then added in very vigorous fashion and more careful writing than usual OH PLEASE. I folded the note and addressed it to the Vicar and walked out of the front door again and down the road to the church. There was a board in the sooty cat-yard beside the west door and I managed to read the times of services. There was an early Communion on Mondays at 6.30 a.m., so I pushed the note under the church door rather than on to the notice board in the porch where he might miss it. Then I walked back, up the gravel again and once more into the front hall. I was a bit put-out to see no light now in the consulting room and coughing and humming and curtain-drawing noises from the sitting-room. But still I made no great efforts at secrecy. I went sedately up the stairs and when I remembered that I had locked my bedroom door on the inside I simply flung open Grace's door alongside it. I marched through, not even looking to see if she were there or not, or alone, or awake. I stepped out through her french windows along the balcony and in through my own. I didn't shut her windows, either. I felt no concern that they might break, that she might catch pneumonia. I felt no interest or guilt at my nastiness or hostility. I lay down and listened to the heavy sound of the bolts being drawn across the front door beneath me and when a second later the dental illumination outside my balcony went out prepared, as I say, to lie awake until the dawn.

I don't really know whether I heard Uncle HB's voice or saw his car first because there I was standing at the window looking at it and hearing the voice below at exactly the same time. I must have been still asleep as I jumped out of bed, my eyes still not properly open as I peered out. But there was a feeling of relief and joy in me that seemed to have been there for quite a time – and the oddest feeling too that all things today would be well.

I put on my shoes and went and hung over the banisters.

He was talking to Mrs Rose who was in her white overall and giving him the confident straight look of a professional about to do fearful but necessary things. "What a silly mistake," Pen was saying smiling at her as if she was the prettiest and most enchanting thing he had seen for years.

"Oh not at all," she was answering brightly. "We're all a bit scatty about Jack's arrangements. He brings home so *many* friends."

"Of course I imagined Bill Green would have said something – long-standing outing – rather vague chap – ha ha ha."

They both laughed indulgently at the thought of father forgetting to tell them that I was leaving them on the Monday a.m. and not in the evening, Uncle Pen knowing perfectly well that father had probably forgotten whether I was coming back at all and would have taken some time to notice had I not.

"I do hope you don't mind – now that we are here?"

"Not at all. Not at all. Jack has Grace Gathering here to keep him happy." (Pen gripped the end of the banister.)

"Um yes."

"Actually we haven't seen much of little Bilgie. She went off to bed early last night. Locked her door. I believe she went to church. There was a little note – I expect she's about now – " She looked vaguely in the direction of the stairs from behind her dentist's mask. She had some sort of sharp thing in her hand again and from behind her in the surgery that dreadful gurgling noise of the pink water could be heard. I saw darling Uncle HB's knuckles whiten on the rail.

"It's all right," I called. "Just coming."

163

"Oh, there you are."

"I'm nearly ready."

"Oh. Super. Sorry not to have seen you, Marigold. See you again. Welcome anytime if you don't mind us being so quiet."

"Thankyouverymuchforhavingme."

"I must get back to my patient."

"I've had a lovely time."

"Good show. 'Bye now." She vanished into her surgery and shut the door and I said, "Oh — " I had wanted to tell her about the amber beads and that she could have them and where they were. I remembered the trace of softness and niceness in her yesterday when she mentioned my ma, and her saying in a way I hadn't thought her capable of, "No — *not* luck". I remembered that I had spent the hostess's present money on the bus fare. But a great whistling came out of the opposite door across the hall which meant that Mr Rose was at the drill again fixing the infected flaps and I saw poor Uncle Pen now rigid with distaste and sweating. "Come *on*, Marigold."

"Just coming."

"Get moving."

"All right I won't be long."

I dashed for the bathroom and took off the black dress and washed with other people's soap and flannels and towels. In a wall cupboard I found somebody's comb. I drew the line at any of the row of toothbrushes though they were in excellent condition and included a range of electrical ones, too. I put the dress back on and went back to my room for the fur coat and put on my tights which had been stuffed down my front all night and were now dry.

"Come *on*," called Uncle Pen.

I looked at the room and decided against making the bed whatever Paula would have said.("Take off the blankets, sheets, pillowslips, fold them rectangular. It's manners in guests.") On the landing I paused a second outside Grace's door. I had a great longing suddenly to go and say goodbye. I remembered the way she'd got me to bed after all that gin. The trip to Marks and Spencers. Perhaps she hadn't known I was invited this weekend after all. And what if she had been rolling about the kitchen on Sunday morning with Jack? Maybe she liked him. It was difficult

164

to know anything about Grace. Jack clearly wasn't good enough for her but maybe she really did like him. I should have liked to talk to her, and a very slow, sad, miserable feeling welled up in me as I stood there, almost as if I was never going to see Grace or Jack or anybody again.

"Bilge, come ON."

"Thank God we're out of that," Uncle HB said on the steps. "Come on quick." He held a back door of the car open for me and went round like a chauffeur to the driver's seat, blowing with relief, "My word. Glad to get away from that. Don't like telling lies. You idiot of a girl. Fearful woman."

"Why'm I in the back?"

"We're picking up two more."

"Are we? Who? Whoever?"

"Boakeses."

"Boakeses? Does Boakes live round here? There's only one of him."

"No. There's his father. Friend of mine. He and I were going off on this outing anyway. I said he'd better bring Boakes as well since I had to collect you. He seemed to think that I ought to collect you as soon as possible. Very urgent about it he was. Crack of dawn this morning. Though he didn't seem to know where you were, except that it was nearby. Funny business. Lucky I knew the address!"

"Boakes's *father!* However could Boakes's father know I wanted to be collected? I never knew Boakes *had* a father. Oh! Good heavens!"

We had stopped outside a grim, plum-coloured dwelling with a lot of net curtaining, none too clean. On the step stood the Vicar and next to him Boakes reading a book.

"You mean *that's* Boakes's father? That Vicar? I don't believe it!"

"Hullo Boakes. Hullo Boakes," said Pen to each in turn. "Well, I've got her. It's hellish early and I don't know what it's all about. Are we too soon?"

"Not a bit," said the Vicar getting in beside him, "Hullo Miss er — How nice to meet you again. Are you feeling better this morning?"

"Been ill?" asked Boakes (son) getting in beside me and keeping a finger in the page like father does, "Hi."

"Not really. Just hang-over," I said, thinking that two days ago I could never have said anything like that to anyone even if it had been true – "Roses. Awful gin. They give you pints. I say is that your *father?*"

"Oh them," said Boakes. "Whatever did you go and stay with them for? Yes of course it's my father, why not?" He gave an amiable nod and went back to Fletcher's *History of Architecture: the Comparative Method*. He was on the chapter on Cathedrals of the Monastic Foundation. The book was nearly the size of a monastery itself.

The car rolled off through the rainy streets of the town towards Thornaby and Stockton-on-Tees. I settled back on the splendid old leather cushions and nobody spoke.

Then, after a while, it struck me that the silence was very companionable. The Vicar and Pen stared ahead of them through the rain, the windscreen wipers purred and a page of Fletcher was occasionally turned.

"Where're we going?" I asked Boakes.

"Durham," said he.

"Why?"

"For a visit."

"Were you anyway?"

"They were. I wasn't – Oxbridge entrance. Last papers coming up. Work and that. But since you were coming – "

We passed through Darlington – its dreadful black church, its lovely covered market, and out to the wide fields beyond.

"An unconventional route to Durham," said Mr Boakes.

"Oh – I don't know," said Pen and began to sing:

> "And so I went to Darlington,
>   That pretty little town,
>   And there I bought a petticoat,
>   A coat and a gown."

"You'd look well in a petticoat, Edmund," said the Vicar and we all laughed, even Boakes who looked up at me from the monastic foundations and said, "I rather like *your* petticoat, Bilgie. Where'd it come from?"

"Never mind."

"I'll bet it didn't come from Jack Rose's. It's a bit ancient isn't it? I didn't know you had a fur coat."

"Oh it's just an old thing."

"Looks as though it belonged to Queen Lear." He winked at me and began reading again. The sun came out.

And quite astonishingly after the pain of the last days I realised that I was enormously enjoying myself. When we got through Barnard Castle Uncle Pen put his foot down and we went rushing towards Durham at speed. Uncle Pen clenched his curly pipe, up-tilted his nose as we sped in and out of villages with mine shafts beside them and pubs called The Pit Laddie. Snow showers and sun succeeded each other over the fells as we reached high ground, and the trees on the field sides against the stone walls sparkled with frost. Down the winding hill into Durham at length the cathedral stood up all at once before us like a potentate. It rose out of brown woods on the high rock over the Wear. Then it was gone.

"Did you *see* it!"

"Have you never seen it before?" said Boakes.

"Never."

We drove over the arched bridge and there it was again. I could hardly bear it when we parked the car and all sailed into the County Hotel for coffee. I said, "Don't let's be long."

"It'll be there when we come out," said Pen. "It has been for the last thousand or so years. Keep your hair on. Bilge my dear, aren't those rather curious clothes?"

"Let's go up right away," I said.

"Not till I've got through this," said the Reverend Boakes and drew up a great plate of pork pie and tea-cakes. "No breakfast," he said. "Early Communion" (He nodded over at me). "We have the whole day before us – my dears, the whole day! Not a meeting, not a service, not a Boy Scout jumble sale, not a marriage, con-fession or Holy Unction – yes please, chocolate biscuits – not a blessed thing except sheer enjoyment," and he licked his fingers like a baby. "Makes up for everything – day like this."

"And we'll have wine for luncheon," said Pen.

There are days that you remember as perfect and which in fact were nothing of the kind. They grow better for the telling and more beloved with the years. For example, to hear Paula go on about her childhood you'd think Dorset had never had a rainy day, all the harvest dripping gold and garlands round each cottage door. I love to hear her carrying on about it, because it does mean something; but I know, and she knows, too, if she would only examine herself, that it is all in fact not so. She has manufactured something – a mood, an atmosphere, a haze which is not there, like the sepia in the photos of her little sisters in their straw hats on her sitting-room mantelpiece. It is quite possible to manufacture a memory completely – as I have pointed out to her on Thursday evenings for so many years. This is known between us and to father, too, though I'm not sure that he really understands it being himself incapable of colouring the truth with the very faintest of tints – as saucer stories.

A saucer story is descended from something years ago when we were all three very happy – the reason has gone, and that's interesting, too. Probably father's exam results were even better than usual or perhaps it was the day they realised that if I put my mind to it I really could read, or perhaps it was when I was at long last better from the beastly measles, or when we'd had the letter from the psychologist to say that although I looked and behaved so dotty my IQ went right off the chart – whatever it was, we were all fooling about washing up and laughing in Paula's private kitchen and Paula began to sing. Then Paula began to do daring things with the china, like flinging it into the air for me to catch. Every time she'd washed a plate – whee! she went, and it spun into the air.

I caught each one because I just had to, and father stopped singing and stood there looking grave. Paula, seeing his face, suddenly picked up the last saucer which was a good one – Spode or something – and whirled round the kitchen with it and then hurled it into space. And I caught it. How, goodness knows. I nearly dropped it. I caught it, dropped it and caught it again and we both dissolved in helpless laughter.

Well, it isn't all that funny if you weren't there, but somehow or other it had a very tremendous and delightful effect upon us and was ever called thereafter "The Night You Dropped the Saucer".

Yet I didn't drop the saucer. It was a fabrication – a manufactured event. "D'you remember the saucer?" we say – and dissolve with laughter. And yet absolutely nothing had happened.

Now the visit to Durham with Uncle Edmund Hastings-Benson and the two Boakeses was just the opposite, in that many things happened – coffee in The County, the wandering walk together up the cobbled hill and over the cathedral close; the time inside the Cathedral where we stood in the nave and the wind blew through the giant pillars from the south door to the north like wind in a forest. Then there was lunch: turkey, stuffing, two kinds of potatoes, sprouts not too long cooked, gravy, red-currant jelly followed by a *good* plum pudding, and a bottle of claret that cost pounds. Then there was evensong in the cathedral – all dark but for the pools of light round the choir stalls, and voices of angels, white ruffs, gold windows. Then we all went out to tea.

These events were all usual. Other people all around us were doing the same things. Yet the memory of them doesn't come up with a name for what went on. It was just a series of things that were important and beautiful and namelessly good, an experience proof against nostalgia, proof against the distortions of time. An experience one is the better for having had even when the brain grows soft and slow and can't remember whether it has just locked the door or was just about to do so. Or if not why not, or if so why. Like Old Price and the zeppelins.

"It has been the most *heavenly* day," said the Reverend. We walked in a line across the Galilee Chapel, away from the dust of the Venerable Bede, the tomb which the angel with a talent for carving in marble had once visited by night with just the right adjective. "A *heavenly* day." We walked out across the huge peaceful cloister towards a low wide tunnel with shallow cross-vaulting and trees creaking their branches in the woods at the other end. We all walked through the woods to a tea-place. It stood out on stilts over the river. There was a coal fire.

The table cloths were clean and red checked, we got a table in the window and the tea and cakes and hot tea-cakes and home-made strawberry jam were brought quickly. Below us rushed the wide brown river, fading in the winter afternoon. Boakes kept on with Fletcher's *Architecture* occasionally looking over his gold specs to hand up his cup. Mr Boakes and Uncle Edmund peacefully munched and in my sables I poured out.

"Time to go." Uncle HB left a colossal tip and we got into the Rolls waiting at the foot of the cathedral hill and went bowling away.

"Uncle Pen," I said when we'd dropped the others, "I love you so."

He looked pleased, rather surprised. "For why because?"

"For rescuing me. For taking me with you. For not asking questions. For not fussing father or Paula."

He sang the song about Darlington again, and petticoats and then said in his funny, old-fashioned Oxford voice, "Matter of fact old thing, why didn't you send for Paula?"

"Oh — the fuss. I don't know."

"I can see you wouldn't send for your father of course — "

"Well of course not. He'd have been — well, anyway he can't drive."

"Ah.

"Bilgie," he said.

"Yes?"

We were through Teesside now and off along the coast beyond Skinningrove and Brotton — nearly home. "Bilge — er. Hum."

"Well, what is it?"

"Well, I just forgot to tell you something. Should have mentioned it before. Paula won't be there when you get back."

"Won't be there? Whyever not?"

"She's gone away."

"Look," I said, "For heaven's sake! Is this one of those Victorian children's books and you're breaking the news about death or something?"

Then — we had reached the front door of father's House — I went ice cold all over beneath my black clothes. "Oh my God!" I said, "Oh my God!"

Chapter 23

HE PURSED HIS lips and began to smooth his hands over the steering wheel, regarding them with deep thought, and I leapt from the car and up the steps and flung through the door of father's study without knocking – coaching or no coaching, he must be disturbed.

"Where's Paula?"

Miss Bex was there. She was sitting alongside father on the saggy old sofa leaning a little towards him. The chess board had been moved on to the top of the heaps of papers on the desk and instead on the chess stool there stood a tray of tea with the best china.

She leapt up like a thing on wires and the look in her eye was the look of the classroom. She didn't say "Go out this minute and come in again properly," but it was as if she had. She stopped herself but noticed that I had noticed.

"Where's Paula?"

"My dear – " Father got up and wafted his arms about. "Miss Bex – "

"Where is *Paula?*"

"Please speak to Miss Bex."

"Hullo Miss Bex. Where is Paula – "

"Paula has had to go home," said father.

"Home? What home?"

"Home to Dorset. For a while. A – a family matter."

"But she didn't say! She didn't tell me a word! When I left on Saturday."

"It all – blew up – on Saturday. She left on Saturday evening."

"Oh heavens!" I collapsed somewhere. "Oh Lord – I thought she was – "

Pen lumbered in grumbling, then said, "Evening Miss Bex. Now what William?"

"Oh we'll manage, we'll manage. Housekeeper back today. And cook. And Miss Bex has very kindly – "

"Just standing in," said Miss Bex with a gleam of teeth, "and I think we all need a nice cup of tea, don't you? This will be cold. Marigold dear – a nice fresh pot for your father."

Father said, "Well – the boarders are beginning to arrive. I'm afraid I must be about outside. Without Paula – "

"I'll do it," I said, "I'll check them in. Miss Bex can find herself some more tea." It sounded rude and I meant it to be.

"Yes indeed," said Miss Bex, not a hair revolving. "*And* cook the supper."

"Er – I have Boys' Supper. The cook is here."

"Then Marigold and I shall have supper together."

"I think – " Father looked utterly lost. It was clear to everyone that Bex ought to go. It was clear to Bex, it was clear to everyone that Pen and I urgently wanted to hear what had happened. It was clear to everyone that boys were arriving tumultuously outside in the hall and that a new boy back for the first time after his first half-term was out there crying and his father having a rough time of it. To three of us it was clear that this boy was little Posy Robinson who loved Paula even more than hamburgers with Heinz tomato which she always gave him when he yearned for home. It was dazzlingly clear. But Miss Bex grinned on.

Pen after aeons said however, "Miss Bex. Might I be allowed to drive you home?" I think it was the only time I heard him speak unenthusiastically on this sort of subject. He picked up her camel-hair coat and father and I fled. But it was obvious to me at this moment as of course it should have been long ago that she was fighting for something and would be back.

I gathered up Posy Robinson in the hall and took him up to Paula's kitchen and cooked him a hamburger with Heinz tomato while father took his father into the study to calm him down. I sat Posy on the San. bed – he is only eleven and very small – and dealt with a long string of boys coming to see Paula to tell her things. Some wanted to tell her things about forgotten bits of their clothing, some about their Half Term and some were carrying the usual presents. One or two of them left the presents on spec. and one or two said that I could have them if she didn't come back.

"Whatever d'you mean?" I said. "Of course she'll come back. Good gracious! The House would fall down without Paula." I said it loud so that Posy Robinson could hear me through the door and also so that I could hear it myself.

"Where she gone then, Bilge?"

"Down to Dorset. Some trouble at home. She'll be back soon."

"I don't feel so good, Bilge," said one of them. "I'm hot. I've got a cough."

"Well you'll have to get rid of it," I said. "Nobody's allowed to be ill till Paula's back. I've got my last exams at the end of the week. I can't be a matron."

"I don't feel so hot either," called Posy. "At least I do. I feel boiling. And I'm shivering all over." I looked through the door at him and saw that he wasn't eating the hamburger. Funny.

Another boy came in with one of those orange-tree plants whose leaves all drop off about Christmas. The leaves were already dropping off.

"Hullo," I said, "Hetherington. Paula's not here. She's – "

"I know," he said, "This could wait for her if it was watered. She's all right is she?"

"Of course she's all right. You're all mad. Just because Paula's not set her foot out of the school premises for about seventeen years you think she's part of the brickwork."

"Sorry," he said, "It's just I'm feeling a bit awful. My mother wasn't sure whether to send me back. I'm sort of hot and I can't stop shivering."

"Beware of self pity," I said, but with an uneasy sort of twinge. "Have you got a cough?"

"Yes. And I've got a rash." He began to give a demonstration of the cough. His cheeks I saw were vermilion. The other boy who

173

had gone through to talk to Posy took up the theme and they coughed for a time in horrible harmony. I ran in.

"I can't eat this hamburger," said Posy, beginning to cry.

"Sit still all three of you," I said and got the thermometers. Spavin and Hetherington were 102, Posy was 104. I said, "Right. Into bed all three of you. You've got the measles."

"My dear, we can't be sure until the doctor comes," said father.

"Yes. One thing I do know is measles. Posy certainly has. Spavin and Hetherington perhaps."

"Spavin, Hetherington and Robinson?"

"And Bell, and I think Bancroft. But theirs may be flu."

"My dear — let's not look on the black side."

There was a knock on the door. It was Easby — a very delicate boy with a bad chest who didn't play games. "Oh, sorry sir, I was just looking for Paula."

"Matron is not here at present."

"Oh. It's just I'm not feeling very well. I can't stop shivering."

And the evening wore on. I got eight in the end, two definite measles, one probable measles and the rest a very nasty variety of flu — or measles brewing. I got the definites into the two special beds in the Sick Room (Easby and Posy) and the possibles all into the San. I moved my stuff into Paula's quarters for the night. I rang the doctor and father rang all the other Houses for the loan of a matron or assistant matron or a master's wife or an anyone, and with absolutely no success. School House had had a measles before the Half Term and now had two more. Also about nine with flu. Into the other Houses droves of boys were staggering, shivering or coughing and covered with spots. Everyone was worked to death.

"Is Rose back yet?" father asked, looking in at nine o'clock after seeing the doctor out.

"He's not been in here."

"Not in his room either. Nuisance. What about Terrapin?"

"I've not seen him."

"Perhaps they've got it. Devilish nuisance. Oxbridge finishes at the end of the week. Thursday/Friday isn't it? The parents should have telephoned. I'll telephone them."

"Yes." I was changing sheets and boiling kettles.

"You can't manage alone, Marigold. You've the last Oxbridge papers coming up yourself."

"I can tonight. Perhaps tomorrow – "

"I'll help you tonight," he said, "I'll just go and get Boakes. He can sit in my study till bedtime and then take on Rose's job – seeing to lights out and such like. I could do with a good junior assistant master."

"I could do with Paula."

The next morning I said it again, "Look, I needn't go in to school today. It's only revision for Oxbridge. But we could do with Paula."

"I must take prayers."

"Father – look. Couldn't we tell Paula? Was it that urgent, whatever she went to Dorset for? She'd be knocked sideways if she knew all this was going on without her."

We both knew, too, that she would be wild with fury if she knew that I was nursing three measles and now ten flus three days away from my final entrance papers. The days before exams she had always cossetted me – or the nearest thing to cossetting that Paula ever did. Nor would she think me in any way capable of doing her job.

"Can't we ring her up?"

"I'm sorry to say we can't," said father, and went out.

"Oh Boakes!" I said, "what's got into him? Whatever d'you think happened?"

"It was a clash of wills," he said. He was filling water bottles prior to going to a Chemistry Practical. "Or so I hear."

"What, between father and Paula! Rubbish!"

"Not between your *father* and Paula." He gave me a long look.

I said, "What if I just said, 'I'm going to school'? He'd have to ring her then? Whatever went on while I was away? I think I'll just walk out."

"You can't," said Boakes. "Not with Easby so bad. The doctor's coming in at ten. You'll have to be there then – your father's teaching."

"But I'm not a servant. I'm not a nurse. Why should I? I know

175

nobody expects me to get into Cambridge but – ”

“They do. You will,” said Boakes, “Take these bottles and then go and wash down Robinson. He’s 105.”

The day passed in five minutes. The doctor took Easby to hospital and promised a district nurse. The district nurse didn’t come – worked off her feet in the town where the flu was flying free. Two parents of the less afflicted patients arrived to wrap their sons in blankets and cart them away. That left only ten, mostly flu, but Posy’s measles were now far too hot to move. Father sat up that night and the next day shared the work with Boakes and the district nurse who turned up for an hour while I went into school to get some books to try and revise from before Thursday. The Wednesday night I said I would do and father said there would definitely be a night-nurse to help me by then. I slept from tea time to nine o’clock and then went up to Paula’s to settle in for duty. I did my rounds (Posy rather better) made some coffee, spread my books around me and sat down to work over Paula’s fire and fell fast asleep again.

I woke at two to hear one of the boys shouting and dashed into the San. feeling terrified, a murderess, but found Boakes there holding a bowl. No night nurse.

“OK Bilge. Don’t worry. It’s only Spavin. Trying to eat. Fool. Make some tea for us.”

I ran down the line of beds and found the rest of the patients asleep – the measles ones with faces like sunsets – flew back and made tea, which was ready by the time Boakes had cleared up. We both drank the tea and felt a bit better.

“Isn’t Rose back yet?” I asked him. “D’you have to do it all?”

“Rose is back but he’s a bit odd.”

“A bit odd? Flu?”

“No – shut himself in his room. Says he’s got Oxbridge.”

“You’ve got Oxbridge too. I’ve got Oxbridge. What about Terrapin?”

“Terrapin isn’t back. I suppose he’s got it.”

“I hope he hasn’t. He’s all alone. Did you know Terrapin lives pretty well all alone? In a great Hall. Only an old char.”

“Oh – he’ll survive.” Boakes stretched himself.

“Don’t you like Terrapin?”

"Well – he's mad isn't he?"

"If you knew what he'd been through. About his father – "

"Being a Battle of Britain pilot?"

"No. He was a pierrot."

"A *pierrot*? Whatever's a pierrot? That's not the tale that goes around."

I said, "Oh, I do wish Paula were back. I'd ring her myself if I knew where she'd gone. Father's so weird about it."

Boakes gave me the queer look again. "Have you tried to find where she's gone? Her address must be somewhere."

"I only know it's Dorset. I don't like to go looking through all her things. She hardly ever gets letters anyway."

"Is that her family in the photo? Maybe there's an address on the back."

We carefully disembowelled the photograph but there was nothing on the back of it except names: Eddie, Dickie, Hepsi and Self. Harvesting.

"They look a nice lot," said Boakes.

"Can't think why she ever left them and stayed here all this time, can you, Boakes? I often ask her. I mean she must be lonely. She'll be more lonely after I've gone to Cam – well, to wherever I get in. I won't get to Cambridge now," I said mournfully.

"Beware of self pity," said Boakes. "What about me? I'm doing no revision either. Mind, nobody's expecting me to get in at all. I had a job even to get old Pen to let me apply."

"Father says you'll get in," I said sleepily. I put my feet up on Paula's couch and shut my eyes. "He's not sure of Jack Rose but don't tell anyone. Terrapin of course will get some fantastic Award as well, that's if he turns up for the exam." The room began to swim about and I sat up. "Help – I'm going to sleep again."

"Sleep," said Boakes pushing me back and covering me up, "I'm here." I watched him for a while with his feet on the table, his glasses on his nose-end, quietly turning the pages of *The Comparative Method* which had absolutely nothing to do with his work and unperturbed by the heavy breathing of the sick through the open door.

I woke up early in the morning and found Boakes asleep, flung backwards in the chair, his glasses on the table and looking very peaceful. I looked at him for a long time. I went into the San. then and the Sick Room. Two boys were awake and talking, the rest asleep. I went to look at Posy who was awake but quiet and I felt him and he was cooler.

"You're over the worst, Posy."

"I'm OK."

"D'you want anything?"

"No. I'm comfy. Well – "

"What?"

"Could I have a hamburger?"

"No you couldn't. But you can have some toast. And a cup of tea."

"I could eat a hamburger. I know I could. I'm hollow." His eyes were immense and he looked very thin. "Is Paula back?"

"Not yet."

"Never mind," he said, "you're almost as good," and turned over and slept.

I felt very happy all of a sudden and tucked him in. I felt great satisfaction about his being well and I patted his pillows and tucked him in a second time. I felt like kissing him, he looked so sweet, but it didn't seem quite the thing. I drew up one of the blinds and looked out on the dark cold morning. It was just getting light and there had been a fall of snow making the roses lumpy and ugly and the herbaceous border queer and plump. The paths were icy.

Then near the wall I saw something very eerie and strange. A shadow of a tree with no snow on it began to move. The tree moved all the way along the wall and across the arch in the wall and over the grass. Under the windows of the long dormitory it stopped, and I found myself stepping back a bit from the window to be less in view.

The shadow of the tree stopped moving and it wasn't a shadow but a woman. It was Mrs Gathering all draped and looped in cloaks like someone out of a William Morris painting. A bad William Morris painting. Her big pale face was lifted up to the boarders' windows and she stood there a long time before turning and gliding off and out of sight. I thought I had never seen such a hapless, hopeless sight – such a big, soft boneless *old* woman – forty-five if she was a day. She looked like a sort of seedy priestess, a sorrowful, sorrowful shade. Not in one thousand guesses would you have guessed she was a Headmaster's wife.

I worked all day, that day the Thursday, at home, and a nurse appeared and an assistant master's wife. Father said he'd do the night duty but I said I would. Posy was better now and in with the others in the San. and the Sick Room beds were empty. I could sleep in there and hear through the door, I said. Nobody was bad now, though Posy still groggy and called out a bit.

"No, no," said father, "I've found an old bird – Mother Gamp woman – who says she'll night nurse and I am free, too, and Boakes is in charge on the Boys' Side."

"What about Rose?"

"Oh he's gone over to School House. He's needed there, Captain of the School and all that, while the Headmaster is away."

"Headmaster *away*?"

"Yes – this bad business."

"What bad business?"

"Oh – " he looked uncomfortable, "don't bother about it now. We'll talk after your Oxbridge."

"For goodness sake father, what bad business?"

"Well, Terrapin."

"Terrapin? But he's in our House!"

"Yes but – "

"What?"

"Well, he's run off with Grace Gathering."

As he said it the phone rang and he answered it thankfully and I stood there with everything in the room looking at once sharp and watchful and unforgettable. I knew that whenever I saw the study curtains pulled back like that in a loop or the Botticelli Primavera with invitations stuck in the frame to the end-of-term concert, or the cat stretching pin-point on all four toes, its red, fiddle mouth, its white point teeth, they would say to me only this: Terrapin has run off with Grace Gathering.

"But he hardly knew her!"

Father said, "Of course. I'll come across at once. Yes."

"And it's his Oxbridge."

"I must go, Marigold. There's – "

"And he hated her. She hated him. You could tell. She couldn't get him. That's why she hated him."

"There's some more trouble. Worse," said father. "We'll talk later." His face looked greenish, bewildered, beyond help as he wound himself into his mufflers. He looked at me for a minute as if he might say something, and then he went out.

Chapter 24

I MET BOAKES in the hall outside but I walked right past him and he only caught up with me right over in the Boys' Side by Paula's stairs. He had looked through the study door as I left and seeing no father had turned back.

"Bilge, there's no need."

I stopped and began to trace over the drawing pins with my finger on Paula's green baize door. "There's an old woman here to night nurse. There's no need for us tonight. We're off duty. She's a bit peculiar but – "

"I want to do it," I said. "Send her home."

"Don't be silly. It's the first exam tomorrow afternoon. You need a sleep."

"I want to be in Paula's."

I went up to Paula's sitting room to tell the night nurse she could go. "The doctor recommended – " said Boakes. "Your father was very insistent. You – "

I went in and said to the broad, rusty back spreading itself over Paula's rocking chair, "I'm so sorry. There has been a change of plan. I shall be on duty here tonight. There's a mistake," and the old bird turned and smiled and was Mrs Deering.

"EEEh dear," she said. "It's 'er of the bus. Well I never. What's this about changes?"

There was a sort of smell in the room of unwashed clothes. Her face had bristles on it and the creases in it very deeply and

181

greasily marked. Her hair was greasy too and as usual she was eating – this time sucking a sweet.

"Have you heard the news?" she said. "He's gone off with her."

"Who's this?" said Boakes. "D'you know each other?"

"We keep on – sort of running across each other," I said.

"Bilge," one of the measles shouted and Mrs Deering smiled. She looked as if once seated she would take very careful thought about disturbing herself.

"All right," said Boakes, "I'll go."

I saw Paula's suitcase on the floor beside her. "I brought it back," she said and closed one eye.

"What d'you mean?"

"The – things – you left in the tower. Your – clothes."

"I didn't know – "

"Not very grand pyjamas. Still, I don't suppose you were – ?"

"Shut up."

"He's gone off with another one now. Oh you're well out of it dear. He has a nasty streak. Mind, he did come after you next morning."

"Be quiet."

"He got the bike out again in the morning and went off to that Jack Rose's. She said – the new one – she told me you'd just left with your uncle and some old vicars when he got there. He stayed on there a bit. Then he brought her – this other one to t'Hall back."

"I don't want to hear."

"Back in to t'tower."

Boakes came in and there must have been something in my face because he said, "Whatever is it? D'you really want her to go?"

"Yes."

"All right. Then she shall. Do you mind too much," he asked Mrs Deering, "can you tell us what we owe you? We think we can manage now. It was really the last couple of nights we needed someone."

"Well, well," she said, "and I'm usually timely. Eight pounds."

"Yes. All right. Where's Paula's petty cash, Bilge?" He went

182

out to find the money and Mrs Deering leaned down in the rocking chair and flung open Paula's case with all my awful clothes in – the ginger zig-zags, the old winceyette pyjamas. "There," she said, sitting back. I scooped them out and ran out of the room and came back with the heap of black clothes and bundled them into the suitcase.

"I've seen that coat many a time," she said. "You looked a treat. Climbing on that bike in it in the middle of the night."

I thought I was going to cry, but Boakes came back and gave her the money and saw her and the suitcase to the door. I don't think I moved one eyelash until he came back.

"Of all the creepy old horrors. Wherever did you pick her up? She's like Sycorax. The Furies. She's terrible. She could really mess anyone up. She's *wicked*."

I said then "I must go a minute," and without stopping for a coat I picked up two of Paula's carrier bags and ran as fast as ever I could out of the sick room, through the Private Side, out and down the steps through the drive and caught up with Mrs Deering as she approached her bus stop.

I called, "Hey." The broad black figure stopped. "It's our suitcase. The Matron's suitcase. Can I have it back? I've brought some carriers."

At first I thought she wasn't going to take any notice. A bus was coming up and she was smiling. "Going to me daughter's," she said. "Well it makes a change."

"Please!"

"Well fancy you bothering! I'd have thought you'd be only thinking of what's happened. They've gone off together you know. London, likely. They won't find neither of them in a hurry there. Mind his family's always been a bit funny. The father being a medium and Swedish. Lovely looking though. And the mother."

The bus had stopped. I grabbed the suitcase, shovelled the clothes into the paper bags and flung them under the stairs on the bus as she heaved herself aboard. I saw the sweet, soft folds of the sable coat sticking out of the top of one of them beside somebody's sticky child's push-chair.

"*She* were a lovely girl, now. The new one," said Mrs Deering. "Well you can't blame him can you?" There was some delay in the bus getting started for quite a lot of people were getting off and Mrs Deering was blocking up the door. As they tried to get past her she leaned over to me and said, "There's not much *I* don't know, dear."

I turned away and carried the empty case back home, thinking about what she had said and sat down in Paula's sitting room looking straight in front of me. The housekeeper had been in with the supper for the Sick Room and there was a bit of conversation going on in there, even some laughs. They were all much better. Boakes was nowhere to be seen and there was no sign of supper for me. In a while, I thought, I'll go and heat up some baked beans or something on Paula's stove, but I didn't. I sat on until how long after I don't know, the phone rang.

It was Pen for father. Was he with me?

No.

Later it rang again. It was Puffy Coleman to send good wishes to Posy Robinson – also to see if father was with me.

No.

Still I sat on. The sounds from the San. ceased. I went in and tidied up and put the lights out and sat on. At half-past ten father rang. He was over at the Headmaster's taking charge of School House. Could Boakes and I manage?

"Of course."

"You've got that old bird?"

"We're fine."

"Darling," he said (the first time ever), "I know it's your Oxbridge tomorrow."

"I'd forgotten."

"Don't sit up. Don't work late. Forget the sick room."

"They're all all right," I said, "All asleep. Couldn't Jack Rose come back over here now? It's Boakes's Oxbridge, too tomorrow. I know it's Rose's as well, but Boakes is tired. He's done such a lot."

There was a silence, then he said, "Jack Rose isn't here, dear. He's, he's gone off."

"But it was *Terrapin* who went off."

"Jack Rose has gone off too."

"But they can't *both* have gone off with Grace Gathering?"

184

"Marigold," said father, "I think you'll have to know something. Rose has gone off with Grace's mother."

"Hullo?" he said after ages, "Marigold? Are you still there? I suppose you're a bit – shocked. I know that I – "

I didn't say anything at all.

He suddenly shouted at the top of his voice, "Oh Marigold – for God's sake find Paula."

I set about systematically taking every single thing of Paula's to pieces. I began with the top left-hand drawer of her desk and worked downwards to the bottom – across the middle knee drawer, then down the right-hand side. I found nothing but House stuff – medical records, notes, handbooks, bits and pieces like sealing wax and safety pins and paper clips. In one drawer I found a folder and a box held together with elastic and I opened them without a qualm and found inside all kinds of things of mine: my first red dancing slipper when I was four (that hadn't lasted long, I was like an elephant) a lock of hair stuck on a card and labelled "Marigold's curl. First hair cut" and the date. There was my weight card from when I was born to three months. In the folder were all my really pathetic efforts at writing and colouring from about four to ten – all just about unreadable, and some feeble drawings. She'd labelled them Marigold's Progress – also all dated. Then there were my music certificates and my O level certificate (I'd been wondering where that was) and two letters I'd written to her years ago when father and I had had four days in Scarborough. There was another box with a few letters in it and I grabbed it thinking that here at last there would be an address, but they appeared to be only from father ages ago when he had had to go to some Classics conference at Oxford. They seemed to be all about House matters but they were carefully tied up with pale pink ribbon.

After the desk I looked everywhere – all through her dressing table, her wardrobe, her bookcase, her table drawers. I looked in old handbags, the box she keeps her stiff nursing collars in. There was not one hint of where she had come from in all the collection. It struck me that for the seventeen years of her life here there was very little to see at all — no records, few books, my mother's old detested sewing machine. She appeared to have taken with her all her clothes. It was like going through the belongings of some old soldier, someone perpetually on duty, someone with no chance and no desire to do anything but serve a cause.

What cause?

I went and lay on one of the now-empty sick room beds — the one that Posy had had, but I'd had the measles so I wasn't worried. At about midnight Boakes looked in. I was lying on top of the blankets with my hands behind my head staring at the ceiling.

"Bilge?" he said, "You all right? You ought to be asleep. Exams tomorrow."

"So have you."

He lay down on the other bed.

"Father's over at School House."

"Yes, I know."

"Have you heard the latest?"

"Yes."

"All this passion," I said, "I suppose I'm pretty blind. Pretty immature for my age. I never guessed."

He got off his bed and came over and lay beside me on mine putting his arm round me and dropping *The Comparative Method* on to the floor with his other hand. "The school is foundering," he said, "I don't know what young people are coming to."

"*Young* people!"

"Bilge," he said, "Were you terribly in love with Terrapin?"

"Eh?"

"Well — he always seemed to be so taken up with you. You could hardly have helped being. Good-looking and all that."

I put both arms round him and thought this is the second time I've been in bed with a boy. There now! — though goodness knows whom I thought I was challenging. I said, "It was Jack Rose really. Till I saw him at home. Terrapin — I'd known him too long."

"Too long?"

"He was ghastly when he was twelve. He was ugly as me."

"You ugly? You're mad. If you want to know," he said, "I've never seen anything more marvellous than you."

"Marvellous?"

186

"In that black dress in the Gothic tea shop in Durham. And marching through the Galilee chapel through the arcading under the crepuscular arches."

I said, "Oh Boakes! Oh Boakes!" laughing and crying at the same time. Boakes tightened his arm and solemnly took off his glasses.

But something came suddenly before my own unspectacled eyes — a vision of the black dress and the soft and luscious sables being scooped out by me into the carrier bags. If one reads or thinks much about the roots of causality and coincidence one is always coming back to the moment of vision, the chicken or the egg. I leapt from the bed, I flew from the room, I fled to Paula's suitcase and I flung it open. There inside the lid was what I had known all the time deep down: vast, black Paula letters saying

        PAULA RIGG

        323, CORPORATION ROAD,

        BUDMOUTH,

        DORSET

"Doesn't sound much like a farm," I cried to Boakes who appeared looking very put-out in the doorway — "Where on earth — ?"

I wrote on a piece of paper, "Come Back. Come Back, Come Back. He needs you so," and I addressed an envelope, found a stamp and ran out to the pillar box in the road opposite the House whose first collection was at 7 a.m. Then I went back and slept soundly in my own bed till morning.

Chapter 25

THE FINAL PAPERS of the Oxbridge were all right. That is to say that the entrance examinations for a place at Girton College, Cambridge did not strike me as being all that. This is what I told people when I came out of the examination room at school anyway. It was a small room called the Hot Plate as the dinners were often kept hot there after cooking and a good smell of shepherd's pie hung about. It was gloriously warm. I was the only candidate and the room was still.

"How was it?" asked Aileen Sykes, wildly friendly, as I came out.

"Fine."

"I say – have you heard – ?"

"I must go now."

The afternoon paper seemed all right, too. It must be queer not being able to do mathematics. Miss Bex was waiting after it was over. "*Now* then, Marigold?"

"Fine," I said and marched off, stuck on my school hat and went home. I went by the promenade and kept my mind intensively on the beauty of the sea, the planes of the white sand and the rocks, the black, broken spikes of the pier. I could see old Pen marching along the sea's edge with Puffy trotting beside him. Pen loped with slow, swooping steps, clenching the pipe. Puffy bobbed. The walrus and the carpenter. They were considering passion. Not oysters. Oysters are supposed to be aphrodisiacs. Did Lewis Carroll know?

They were discussing passion and the shame of St Wilfrid's. I wondered if they'd told Old Price.

"What d'you think, Price? The Head's wife has gone off with the Captain of the School and his daughter with the best Classics brain we've had in fifty years. The Head's in London looking for them all like Mr Bennet. Bill Green is in charge of the School House and his Matron's left him."

"Ah well. There have been these crises. I remember the zeppelins."

"And Marigold Green has been running her father's House. They've all had the flu and the measles and she's messed up her Cambridge Entrance."

"Cambridge entrance? Dear me, do they have girls at Cambridge now? Dear me!"

Had I mucked it up? Had I just – when I let myself think about it – had I just perhaps written my name over and over again on the paper like they say people do sometimes when they're overdone? Or had I turned in blank pages?

No – I was sure I remembered handing Miss Bex pages with writing on them.

"What were they like, Marigold?" Father was briefly back in his study looking for things. Miss Bex was there yet again, pouring tea from a silver pot.

"Fine," I said.

"I just came along to Hold the Fort," said Bex, "and see you got some tea after all your endeavours. And I brought some little cakes."

Father was looking frantically about for papers. "I can find them," said Bex, briskly. "I did a good tidy-up before you came in. Oh I understand these servant problems."

"I've got to go now," I said.

"Don't over-prepare," said Bex.

"I'm afraid I must go, too," said father, "I'm living at the School House just at present, Miss Bex."

"My *dear*! I have *heard*!" She gave him a long, very meaningful look. "But I can stay here. I shall be Of Use. I shall Man the Telephone."

On the stairs Boakes hung about. "Bilge – what were yours like?"

"Oh fine."

We looked at each other without conviction.

The next day was the general paper and I chose an essay called Coincidence. I wrote steadily, easily, fluently, unhesitatingly. I wrote of chess, relating it to mathematics, of the final appropriateness of events, of Shakespeare with reference to *Hamlet*, of *The Tempest* with reference to Sycorax, of the Eumenides, the "Kindly Ones" with reference (veiled) to father, Mrs Deering and the Reverend Boakes. I wrote of truth, and the necessity of it not to be manipulated and veiled in white samite, veiled in black sables, of Terrapin, of Terrapin's versatile father – in philosophical terms of course. I ended with a dissertation on the mathematical peace experienced in the realms of chess, in the pathways beyond accident, coincidence or desire.

I finished half an hour early and took pieces of my hair and plaited them carefully in many small pigtails, and when Miss Bex and the Headmistress arrived to let me out there were about thirty orange rat's-tail lashes wagging about my head. They looked surprised.

"*Well*, Marigold. How was it?" said Bex.

"Oh fine."

"Good girl," smiled the Headmistress (Kind and quiet. I like her very much. I felt a heel). "That's a good girl."

"How was it?" said Boakes. "God knows," I said, "Except that I made an ass of myself. I let myself go. Well, no one expects me to get in anyway. What was yours like?"

"I covered some pages with words," said Boakes. "The view of the Abbey from the window was very fine. And comforting."

"Well, it's over and we can forget it," I said. "No one expects either of us to get in."

"Where will you go instead?"

"Oh – I don't know. Teacher-training. Trainee at Marks and Spencer. I love Marks and Spencer. They have wonderful clothes. Has the post come?"

It had, but there was nothing from Paula.

Chapter 26

THE NEXT FIVE days I spent not doing things. I behaved in such a curious way that when I think about it now, at Christmas, I can't believe that such a person ever existed outside the madhouse.

I suppose it was the shock of having finished with school. Believe it or believe it not I had not realised that when Oxbridge was over, school would be over, too, for ever. Five to seventeen. All those years and years and years of bells. Such an age and age of school. Those preps and speech days and Aileen Sykes and Miss Bex. The awful gym lessons. The terrible dinners. The smelly lavatories. The frightful, pitiless games of hockey with me always running the wrong way. The sniggers, the friendlessness. But at the same time the pattern, the plot, the safety was now gone. The plans all made for you, the security of knowing that on Monday come wind or high water you would have to be doing Double Applied. That if anyone wanted you in a hurry they would know for certain you would be in Room Eight, over the Quad. The sureness of what to do next. The sureness that you were not just wasting your time — because you had no choice in the matter anyway. The sureness that free time was precious and that the sands and the sea and the park and the garden had heavenly properties because, like heaven, they were except at certain moments forbidden and inaccessible.

Now I was utterly free. A master's wife and an imported assistant master and Uncle Pen had taken over the House and I was not needed at home. The brief occasions when father came back to deal with the odd essential thing – like Easby's parents who wanted to know why there had been no trained nursing staff in the school when Easby nearly passed away (he was fine now) or when Posy Robinson's mother came over with six rose bushes and a bottle of champagne and a heavenly pair of lamb-lined gloves for me, to thank us – were always marked by the presence of Miss Bex.

The study grew yet tidier; bleaker and bleaker. The chess set was removed first from the fireside stool to the desk, then, when she set to work tidying the desk, elevated to the bookcase. When it was noticed to be on a tilt there, by father, Miss Bex decided to put it sensibly away in a cupboard, and father made no demur at any of this. His shoe-supply disappeared from under his desk, his bottles of rosé from his side desk shelf. Only the Botticelli gleamed at her still with its demon-cold, cruel, Spring, Grace Gathering eyes.

"It's a terrible thing to say," said Bex, the Sunday evening, "but I've never felt I really liked that painting much. I could never *live* with it. It makes me – slightly frightened. More shortbread?"

"I must go now, Miss Bex."

"Now that you are an Old Girl, Marigold, can't you call me Ursula?"

And I spent my time not doing things. I set out to see Mrs Rose. I got a sort of obsession about Mrs Rose. I wanted to tell her about the beads in the pot and say how lovely the food had been; that I was so terribly sorry about Jack going off with Mrs Gathering. I got to the door of the Dentistry in the bus, and then let the bus pass by and ended up somewhere in Billingham in a maze of dingy houses and walked there for hours and then went home. On the Sunday I decided to go and see Mr Boakes and set off again in the same old bus. I got to the church in time, but the sight of the white-haired ladies, all helping each other in, and the dismal clank of the bell pulled by Mr Boakes's little woollen paws filled me with tremendous gloom and I passed by and looked in shop windows, Sunday-locked shops, examining samples of wall-to-wall carpet and imitation leather sofas. Then I went back home again and found I'd missed lunch. On Monday I went over to the Comprehensive, skirted the buildings and stood on the cliff top where the hay-cocks had been and Grace so all-powerful and quiet, holding her wet nails to the ocean. There was nothing there but the loop of wire swinging in the cold wind.

On the Tuesday I went by train to Durham and it rained. The cathedral was cold and draughty and crowded. Children cried and shouted. One — inside in the main aisle — was sucking an ice-cream. In the Galilee Chapel, the tomb of the Venerable Bede looked dark and dreary — a block of stone covering nothing. The tea shop was shut. A card on the·door said Closed for Alterations. There were signs of builders there, a bar being built, a counter for plastic trays.

On the Wednesday — the last day for a telegram from Cambridge if either Boakes or I were to be worthy of inspection (for at Oxbridge, you are only told if you are wanted. If they don't want to see you, you hear nothing.) — on the Wednesday I decided that I would go to Terrapin's.

There was a piercing, cold wind and sleety rain and I got out of the bus, this time in daylight at his broken-down and noble gateway and stood looking up the drive. It was shorter than it had seemed in the dark. You could see from the gate where it curved round to the terrace. The tall swaying trees were only moth-eaten pines. There was a heap of rubbish beside the lodge which had boarded up windows and pieces of wood nailed across the door. I could not see the Hall, not even its tower, and I stood about on the windy empty road and caught the next bus home.

Boakes was in his room when I got back, reading away about the Perpendicular and Decorated, eating a thick piece of Dundee cake. His glasses were crooked. He looked silly and plain. I said, "I suppose no post came?"

"No."

"We haven't got in then."

"It seems not." He smiled imperturbably. "Come and have some tea."

I wandered away downstairs and to the study and found, as usual, Bex sitting on the sofa very close to father and looking appealingly or so she thought into his face. He wasn't actually looking back, but there was something about him that was new. It was a sort of — what? A sort of renunciation, a relinquishing, a giving up. The fingernails were slipping from the precipice, the towel was being handed over — as I watched he began slowly to unravel his muffler. He gave it her and she tenderly patted it away, and I knew what I had been running away from all week and much longer – since I had come back from Jack Rose's, since Bex had installed herself each tea-time, since well! OF COURSE – since Paula had gone away. "She's got him," I thought. That's why Paula left. "He's had it. And so have I."

"There was nothing from Cambridge?" I had to say something and it just came into my head. Nothing on earth would normally have made me show to Bex that I cared. It was just that I had to speak, to break the spell between them, and this came out.

She looked across at me and gleamed with her teeth and said in a horrible, falsely gentle way, "I'm afraid not, dear."

"Was there, father?"

He was fluttered and fussed. "Um – no, dear. No."

"Shall I go?"

"Go?" he said.

"You seemed busy."

"No, no. Of course not."

"Perhaps she could just see about Boakes being in? Couldn't she William? Just see that he can take charge while we're out?"

"Out?"

"Yes dear – your father is coming for a little quiet supper with me. Now that all the exams are over and term ending, there is no real need for him to be in the House."

"I do know that," I said, "I've lived here for some time."

"Marigold," said father, "you're being rude."

"Are you really going out?" I said.

"Well – er – um."

"Of course your father's going out. My dear, your father doesn't go out enough. It is quite ridiculous."

"But it's Thursday."

"Whatever has that to do with it?"

"He never goes out on Thursdays."

"Whyever not?"

"Well, it's his *Thursday*."

Father said, "My dear Miss Bex – Ursula – I'd quite forgotten. So it is."

"Whatever is all this about?"

194

"My dear – I am so very sorry. I always have some very old friends here on Thursdays. Hastings-Benson, Coleman and – er – dear Old Price."

"But really," she said, "this is ridiculous. How long has this been going on?"

"Oh well – many years. Since we were all – "

"But they are all *years* older than you!"

"Yes. Of course. But you see nevertheless we are very old friends."

"And is Marigold in on this little festivity?"

"Not exactly. Not for a while. Not since she was a baby. She always spends – spent – Thursdays with Paula. Oh dear," he said but quite firmly, "I am afraid that this cannot be changed."

Miss Bex went dark red and began to tap her foot and then her hand. It might have been a Hamlet lesson. "But I have prepared a sole," she said, "I should have been told about this."

Father, with his most sweet and helpless smile said again, "I am so sorry." And I felt a gleam of hope as Bex flushed darker yet.

"I've never heard anything so stupid in my life," she said. "You're turning yourself into a fossil – living here, entertaining no one but a lot of old men – your House at sixes and sevens – your helpless daughter – the sooner your atrocious Headmaster and his family sacked the better – senile staff – place go Comprehensive – in Line with the Times. Your servants may walk out on you – this 'Matron'. I will not. Keep your Thursday if you must. I will stay for it."

"Oh Miss Bex," I said, "No one ever stays for it. It is an all-male affair."

"What rubbish," said Bex and put out both hands towards father. "Dear William! Dear Bill." I saw him waver. I saw him hesitate. He is the most easily pleased of men. He blinked. I could hear him think, "She can't really have said all those awful things. I dreamed it." He took her hands.

And I couldn't bear it. I fled. I rushed out of the door with tears behind my glasses blinding me. There was nobody left now. Head down I plunged at the front door and the winter dark, and head down I plunged into Paula striding in from it towards me.

"The Lord Ins Murzy, what's happnin'?"

"Oh, oh."

"My lover, what's happnin'?"

"Wherever have you been? Oh *wherever* have you been? I wrote a week ago. He's getting married. He's marrying Miss Bex. He hates her but she's caught him. Mrs Gathering's gone off with Jack Rose and Terrapin's gone off with Grace Gathering and Boakes and I haven't got into Cambridge and we've had a measles and a flu epidemic and Easby nearly died. Why didn't you get here quicker?"

"I'd gone down to Uncle's farm. The letter missed me. I only got back to Budmouth this morning."

"But it's Father's *Thursday* — and Bex is staying — "

"Ho, she is, is she?" said Paula, "Well in just one minute we'll see. Keep my taxi. Here — here's two telegrams from Cambridge waiting as usual at the post office. Seems nobody cares if I don't. Time immemorial they've been collected. Sittin' there waitin'! One Boakes. One Green. Wait on. Old your 'osses." — and she vanished with her great whoosh of hair into the study. I stood with the telegrams and in seconds Bex was out, with Paula alongside, blazing of eye.

Bex went whirling by into the darkness, and I heard Paula's taxi starting up and driving away.

Paula came back. "Well, there now."

"Oh Paula! She'd asked him to supper. She'd prepared a sole."

"She should look to her own. Here. Quick while I ring Boakes."

In the study father stood and his face was so joyous and young I had to stop for a minute and just look at him. Paula sent for Boakes on the House phone, and as we waited for him she flew about, rushing at the fancy tea tray, reinstating the chess stool, exclaiming at piles of neat papers, flicking matily with her scarf at the Botticelli. "There now," she said to Boakes. "Open them."

I realised that I was standing holding telegrams.

"Left at the post office. Time out of mind. Always left for me to collect. First time I'm not here in seventeen years — forgotten! I always at least remembered to telephone through."

Father looked ashamed. "Paula," he said, "we've been having a very terrible time. I've hardly been at home. Marigold has done splendidly — "

"What has Marigold done?"

"I don't know," I said, "But I've not got an interview at Cambridge. I've got three. 9.30 and 11 a.m. 4.30 p.m. – day after tomorrow signed Peace."

"So have I. Three interviews," said Boakes, re-settling his glasses, "Signed 'Master'."

"My dear, my dear," said father, his face with its lovely smile, "You're in, you're in. If there are Further Interviews they are thinking – ah. Hum – in terms of an Award. A Scholarship. You too, Boakes."

"That's nice," said Boakes calmly as I burst into tears and Paula with a cry of triumph flung herself wildly into father's arms.

Uncle Edmund Hastings-Benson arrived at the same time and stood for a while bewildered. Puffy Coleman coming up alongside, holding a tin of Old Fashioned Peppermint Humbugs for Posy Robinson, let his mouth fall open and forgot to turn sideways. Faint snuffles could be heard beyond as Old Price negotiated the hallstand.

"What's this then, Boakes?" said Pen.

"I think Marigold and I might get Scholarships to Cambridge."

"And," said I, loud and clear, "Paula is going to marry father."

"And Miss – er – Bex?"

"She's eating Dover sole."

"A good fish," said Old Price. "I remember how we missed it in the Boer War. Or was it the other one? That was a terrible business with Africa."

Boakes said he had to ring up his father. Uncle Pen said we would now open Posy's parents' champagne. Puffy said why should not he and Boakes's father and Pen drive me and Boakes to Cambridge for our interviews tomorrow in Uncle Pen's Rolls.

But Boakes – said No. Bilge and I, he said, would really rather prefer to be by ourselves. And to my great astonishment I found that I agreed to this, with a very particular sort of excitement.

Epilogue

THE PRINCIPAL walked right down the stairs with the candidate and out of the front door with her. When the candidate looked slightly surprised, the Principal nodded at her just like anyone. "I'll set you," she said.

"Oh – thank you."

"Do you still say 'set you' 'set you home', Miss Terrapin? I come from your bit of the world you know."

"Yes we do. Yes I did," said Miss Terrapin.

She and Lady Boakes walked across the courtyard, past a fountain. The coloured windows of a chapel hung against the dark. "What a strain these interviews are," said Lady Boakes. "When I had mine I had just caught the flu and my husband – the young man who became my husband – was catching the measles."

"What awful luck."

"No it wasn't." Lady Boakes chuckled. "It was our own silly fault."

Miss Terrapin was at a loss.

"I went to your school you know," said the Principal.

"Oh yes," said Miss Terrapin, "You're on the board – the Honours Board." She put her head back and laughed and two young men passing stopped talking to look at her bright face and curious pink-gold hair. "I saw your name in letters of gold every morning in prayers. The top of the list."

"How ghastly," said Bilgewater.

"Have you never been back?" asked Miss Terrapin.

The Principal had stopped to examine a fountain which she must have been able to examine many times before. It was a very cold day. Miss Terrapin had a train to catch.

"No. I don't seem to have been back. My people moved to Dorset – my father had a chest. Then we have my old father-in-law here in Cambridge, and I have a very ancient Uncle here."

(She's very chatty.)

"We don't go about much," said the Principal, moving on again over the Quad. "Except abroad of course to see the buildings."

(Buildings? She's nuts.)

"With my husband."

(Lord yes of course. Buildings. Old Sir Edward Boakes. Architect-architectorum. Excellentissimus. Magnificissimus.)

"There is an old Mrs Rose I write to at Christmas – a friend of my mother. Retired dentist – "

(Whatever next!)

"Do you know her? Ironstoneside?"

"Er – no."

"You still live – ?" said the Principal.

"At Marston Hall. My father – It's a theatre."

"I've heard I think."

"Experimental."

"Yes."

"Sometimes – well he's a bit of a genius. And sometimes the experiments aren't – well, all that successful."

"No."

"It's a bit scruffy but it's a lovely house. The new estates have reached all up round it now – right up to the terrace. But we've hung on somehow. Mother hated it." (I'm babbling.)

"Your mother – ?"

"Oh she went off."

They stood under the archway of Caius and the Principal said how delighted she had been to meet Miss Terrapin. "You have your father's cheekbones," she said, "and your mother's charm." They shook hands once more, and both looked sensibly left and right before Miss Terrapin attempted to cross the foggy road.

"Is the tower still there?" asked the Principal suddenly.

"No. We took it down. At least the old creature who looks after us – him – made us. She said it would do for us, come down on us if we didn't."

"She would."

"I beg your pardon?"

"Will you tell your father," said Lady Boakes, chin down in her good fur coat like a small owl – "Will you say I'm sorry. About the tower."

"Funny woman," thought the candidate. I wonder why father thought – ? Can't ever have been pretty. She looked hard at Lady Boakes's face and thought it seemed saddish.

"It had to come down," she said kindly. "You see it really was getting unsafe."

"It was always unsafe."

Shall I tell her? thought Miss Terrapin. Can't do any harm. I'm not coming here. I've decided. I don't know when I decided but I have decided. I'm going to RADA – I'll shack up with mother in the Earls Court Road.

"Father was absolutely crazy about you," she said and skipped across Trinity Street. Two cyclists seeing her bounce like a light into Market Square wobbled together in the mist and fell off.

I've done it now all right, thought Terrapin's daughter. Let's hope I've got into RADA now! What a thing to say to Lady Boakes – first woman Principal of Caius and blaa and blaa! She turned and was even more unnerved to see the Principal still standing solemnly on the kerb. You can see she's never done anything silly in her life, thought Miss Terrapin and growing sillier herself she gave a jaunty wave.

Oh help! Oh worse and worse! she thought. I have jauntily waved!

But Bilgewater, across the winter afternoon, waved back.

THE FLIGHT OF THE MAIDENS

Jane Gardam

'Gardam . . . has written another jewel. The tale of the three young women is made with a concentrate of humour and compassion. Gardam is a brilliantly subtle comedian who can keep the reader enraptured until the last page'
The Times

The Flight of the Maidens describes the post-war summer of 1946 – and follows three young women in the months between leaving school and taking up their scholarships at university: Una Vane, whose widowed mother runs a hairdressing salon in her front room (Maison Vane Glory – Where Permanent Waves are Permanent), goes bicycling with Ray, the boy who delivers the fish and milk; Hetty Fallowes struggles to become independent of her possessive, loving, tactless mother; and Lieselotte Klein, who had arrived in 1939 on a train from Hamburg, uncovers tragedy in the past and magic in the present.

'As a celebration of the rites of passage it rings diamond true. It is light, witty, sharp, yet understanding and sympathetic. It is also thoroughly enjoyable'
Scotsman

'Gardam blends memory and imagination, intellect and humour, to evoke unsentimentally a vanished England, setting it in the context of the wider world and capturing the bittersweet excitement of leaving childhood behind'
Daily Telegraph

'Jane Gardam, as ever, shapes her narrative with wit and aplomb . . . intelligent, inspiriting and entertaining'
Independent

Abacus
0 349 11424 2

GOING INTO A DARK HOUSE

Jane Gardam

WINNER OF THE MACMILLAN SILVER PEN AWARD 1995

'Molly Fielding's mother had been a terrible woman . . .'
A terrible woman indeed. One need only look at the old
sepia photograph to see a vision of nastiness. The look of
cunning, the self-satisfied smile, the aura of hauteur as she
watches the little Italian photographer go about his business.
They say the camera never lies, but maybe this one did.
'Going into a Dark House', the title story of Jane Gardam's
passionate collection, brilliantly captures the subtly
subversive qualities of her art. Quietly mesmeric and
beautifully written, these ten stories are a delight.

'Pure delight . . . one perfect story after another'
Sunday Telegraph

'Flawlessly written, with dialogue so angular and sparky,
and descriptions – of landscapes and food – so lovely and
hard edged, that they are a revelation of the extraordinary
effects ordinary language can achieve'
Victoria Glendinning, *Daily Telegraph*

'Jane Gardam's stories are as good as ever'
Anita Brookner, *Spectator*

'Richly imaginative . . . beautifully written'
Evening Standard

'Excellent . . . well worth reading'
Sunday Times

Abacus
0 349 10661 4

MISSING THE MIDNIGHT

Jane Gardam

'These are wise and witty tales impossible to read without smiling . . . "Miss Mistletoe" has the perennial unwanted guest turning the tables on her hosts; "Old Filth" finds two ancient enemies, Hong Kong lawyers both, seeking an eleventh-hour *rapprochement*; "The Zoo at Christmas", a minor masterpiece, reveals that even non-human inmates can celebrate the nativity . . . Gardam never preaches; she is full of surprises'
Time Out

'Plundering ancient English folklore and modern manners for her subject matter, from Green Man to career woman, Jane Gardam has fashioned a dozen sturdy stories with surprisingly dark souls . . . stories that haunt long beyond the word on the page'
Observer

'Christian legend is explored through talking animals; the notion of grace through a man born with a diamond in his neck; obsession is a boy who becomes a bicycle . . . like this, at her quiet best, Gardam is a moving and memorable writer'
TLS

'Arrestingly good . . . *Missing the Midnight* shows off Gardam's talents: her glittering use of colour; her unfussed, economical use of the telling detail'
Daily Telegraph

'Sparkling . . . her simple tales have moral conundrums at their heart, yet are joyous and sensuous in their sheer love of words'
Suzi Feay, *Independent on Sunday*

Abacus
0 349 11017 4

THE PANGS OF LOVE

Jane Gardam

With her customary accuracy, Jane Gardam reveals the
extraordinariness of ordinary people as she deals with the
pangs of love – fulfilled or hopeless, sexual or spiritual,
tortured or hilarious – in these eleven stories.
Paraded here are ladies with a 'thing' about vicars, strange
events happening in ornate downstairs lavatories (and in
ornate upstairs ones), and the English abroad, desperate and
dotty. The glum and impossible Edna haunts the
supermarket – and dispenses an unlikely kiss of life. The
younger sister of Hans Christian Andersen's Little Mermaid
declares her sibling 'very silly' – and turns her story on its
tail, an old maid forms a curious liaison with a tramp, and
small moments of temptation fill hotel rooms as histories
glance briefly off each other.

'A spare and elegant master of her art'
The Times

'Exuberant narration and stylish dialogue; I read it with
relish . . . powerful and haunting'
Penelope Lively, *Sunday Telegraph*

'Marvellously precise sleight-of-hand short stories'
Daily Mail

'All the stories possess a delicacy and economy which leaves
one, having read them, with just the right measure of
pleasurable incompleteness'
Financial Times

'Assured and enjoyable'
Evening Standard

Abacus
0 349 11404 8

THE QUEEN OF THE TAMBOURINE

Jane Gardam

Eliza Peabody is one of those dangerously blameless women who believes she has God in her pocket. She is too enthusiastic; she talks too much. Her concern for the welfare of her wealthy South London neighbours extends to ingenuous well-meaning notes of unsolicited advice under the door.

It is just such a one-sided correspondence that heralds Eliza's undoing. Did her letter have something to do with the woman's abrupt disappearance? Why will no one else speak of her? And why the watchful, pitying looks and embarrassment that now greet her?

'Brilliant'
Sunday Times

'Marvellously subtle and moving'
The Times

'An ingenious, funny, satirical, sad story – vivid and poignant'
Independent on Sunday

'Excellently done . . . manic delusions were never so persuasive . . . very moving when it is not being exceedingly funny'
Anita Brookner, *Spectator*

'Brilliant, wickedly comic . . . masterly and hugely enjoyable'
Daily Mail

Abacus
0 349 10226 0

Now you can order superb titles directly from Abacus

☐	Crusoe's Daughter	Jane Gardam	£6.99
☐	Faith Fox	Jane Gardam	£7.99
☐	The Flight of the Maidens	Jane Gardam	£6.99
☐	God on the Rocks	Jane Gardam	£6.99
☐	Missing the Midnight	Jane Gardam	£6.99
☐	The Queen of the Tambourine	Jane Gardam	£6.99
☐	The Sidmouth Letters	Jane Gardam	£7.99
☐	Going into a Dark House	Jane Gardam	£6.99

Please allow for postage and packing: **Free UK delivery.**
Europe; add 25% of retail price; Rest of World; 45% of retail price.

To order any of the above or any other Abacus titles, please call our credit card orderline or fill in this coupon and send/fax it to:

Abacus, P.O. Box 121, Kettering, Northants NN14 4ZQ
Tel: 01832 737527   Fax: 01832 733076
Email: aspenhouse@FSBDial.co.uk

☐ I enclose a UK bank cheque made payable to Abacus for £ ....

☐ Please charge £.............. to my Access, Visa, Delta, Switch Card No.

☐☐☐☐☐☐☐☐☐☐☐☐☐☐☐☐☐☐☐

Expiry Date ☐☐☐☐   Switch Issue No. ☐☐

NAME (Block letters please) ....

ADDRESS ....

....

....

Postcode ....Telephone ....

Signature ....

Please allow 28 days for delivery within the UK. Offer subject to price and availability.

Please do not send any further mailings from companies carefully selected by Abacus ☐